A ROGUE IN WINTER

A ROGUES TO RICHES NOVELLA

GRACE BURROWES

GRACE BURROWES PUBLISHING

A Rogue in Winter

DEDICATION

To all the lonely rogues and roguettes (I made that word up) biding at the edge of the moor in deepest, darkest winter

CHAPTER ONE

"I ought not to abandon you at such a busy time, Vicar." Mrs. Baker bustled toward the front door with an enthusiasm that belied genuine remorse. "The holidays see you run ragged, but my Eunice has all those children and another one due any day. Tell me I'm forgiven?"

Pietr Sorenson was good at telling people they were forgiven—as any vicar should be—and the peace and quiet Mrs. Baker's annual absence provided was in truth a much treasured holiday gift.

"You are not only forgiven," Pietr said, mustering his kindly vicar smile, "you are wished Godspeed, and my love to your family." He kissed Mrs. Baker's cheek in deference to the mistletoe she'd hung in the foyer, picked up her valise, and escorted her to the waiting coach.

"I've never traveled in such style," she said as a liveried footman lashed her valise to the boot. "My grandchildren will think the queen has arrived."

"They will be more excited to know it's their dear granny, bearing gingerbread, newly knitted socks, and family tales of Christmases past."

Though the Rothhaven ducal traveling coach did qualify as a luxury barge on wheels. Pietr had asked to borrow it on Mrs. Baker's behalf, because the public stage was a penance not to be borne in winter's darkest weeks.

And if some small part of Pietr wanted to know for a certainty that Mrs. B was well and truly off to York for a few weeks... Well, no matter.

A man climbed down from the box while the horses stomped in the snow. He was slim, dark-haired, tallish, and attired in the height of winter fashion.

"Mr. Wentworth." Pietr bowed rather than extend a hand. He barely knew Ned Wentworth and would not presume any sort of familiarity with a member of a ducal household. "Good day."

"Vicar. Mrs. Baker." Mr. Wentworth bowed over the lady's hand, which resulted in a woman old enough to be Pietr's mama *simpering*. "I hitched a ride into the village rather than trudge both directions in this snow. I thought winter in London was a tribulation, but Yorkshire..."

"Worse than Scotland, some people say," Mrs. Baker remarked. "The Vikings were right at home here. I must be off, for the light doesn't last this time of year."

She dipped a hasty curtsey, and Mr. Wentworth handed her into the coach. The coachman saluted with his whip, and the vehicle jingled and clattered down the snowy street.

"I was tempted to nip into York," Mr. Wentworth said. "To go someplace where buildings come in a proper batch, not isolated in a sea of snow. I never thought I'd miss the stink of London's coal smoke or the crowded walkways, but I do. The silence alone this far from civilization is enough to drive a man daft."

The Bible listed commandments, while a vicar developed a list of ailments of the human heart. Homesickness figured somewhere near the top.

"Come in for a cup of tea, Mr. Wentworth. Give the shops an hour to get their parlor stoves roaring. Mrs. Baker always fills the larder with holiday treats before she departs."

Wentworth looked skeptical. "I truly do have errands to run,

Vicar. I suspect the ladies at Lynley Vale wanted me out from under-foot while the decorating got under way. Lord Nathaniel is trying to help, and Lord Stephen is making suggestions, while the footmen have all developed bad hearing. I was one dunderheaded male too many."

That was a falsehood, and right now, watching the Wentworth ducal coach trot out of the village, Pietr was inclined to name it as such.

"You are not a Wentworth by blood, so you banished yourself from what you regarded as a family undertaking. Forget the tea, let's have a tot to ward off the chill. Frequent doses of wassail are how we get through our winters here."

"Wassail?"

"Wassail, toddies, a nip from the flask. Everybody thinks York-shiremen are tough. We're more determined than tough, and we've learned to make our peace with the elements. Inside with you, Mr. Wentworth, and we will see what Mrs. Baker has left me in the way of sweets."

"Jane said I shouldn't underestimate you."

Jane being Her Grace of Walden, a formidable woman who made duchessing look much easier than it was. But then, Jane was married to Quinton, Duke of Walden, and compared to being that fellow's wife, wearing a tiara was doubtless a Sunday stroll.

"You need not estimate me at all," Pietr said, leading the way up the vicarage's steps. "I'm a humble country parson living a placid existence in the bucolic splendor of rural nowhere." He'd meant that observation as a jest, but it had come out sounding a bit... forlorn?

Whiny?

"Pour me a bracer," Mr. Wentworth said, "and you can be my new best friend. I really am not accustomed to this cold."

"Has anybody given you the sermon for southerners yet?" Pietr asked, taking his guest's hat, coat, and gloves. "If leaving home, always dress as if you'll be outside all day, for you might be. Layers of wool are best, and that means two pairs of stockings if possible. Three if you can manage it. Forget vanity. Winter here will kill you if you give it a chance. If you are caught out in bad weather, try to keep moving at a slow, steady pace, provided you can see where you are going. If you sit for a moment to rest, next thing you will close your eyes, and Saint Peter will be offering you a pair of wings."

Mr. Wentworth glanced around the vicarage, which Mrs. Baker kept spotless. The place was less than a hundred years old—thus it was the *new* vicarage—and detached from the church, unlike the prior manse, which was now used for Sunday school, meetings, and fellowship meals.

Like every other durable structure in Yorkshire, the vicarage was a stone edifice. The interior was lightened by whitewashed plaster walls, mullioned windows, and polished oak floors covered with sturdy braided rugs. Darkness in the form of exposed beams, wain-scoting, and fieldstone hearths did battle with light, and on an over-cast winter morning, the gloom was winning.

"The Lynley Vale butler says we're in for more foul weather," Mr. Wentworth observed, following Pietr into his study. "I have never seen snow like you have up here. Acres of snow, waist-deep, and the sky looks like nothing so much as more snow preparing to further bury a landscape we won't see again until July."

"The first winter is something of an adventure," Pietr said, going to the decanters on the sideboard. "Brandy?"

"If you will join me."

Pietr poured two generous servings and passed one to his guest. "The second winter, you realize about halfway through that it's not an adventure, it's a penance. You endure the third winter on the strength of grim resignation, and the fourth winter, you resolve to move south come spring."

Wentworth sipped his drink. "How long have you been here?"

"More than four winters is simply referred to as 'too long' by one not born in these surrounds, though the other seasons are glorious. Would you care for a hand of cribbage? Chess, perhaps?"

Men could not simply sit and talk with one another. Learning that had taken Pietr several years. Women, perhaps because their work was so unrelenting, had the knack of purely spending time in one another's company. Men were more difficult to put at ease.

"It's damned snowing again." Mr. Wentworth's tone was indignant as he took his drink to the window. "Pardon my language, but it snowed yesterday and the day before."

"I would not want to be the bearer of bad news,"—vicars were frequently exactly that—"but it's likely to snow again tomorrow and the next day." Pietr considered his drink, though really, consuming spirits this early in the day, and so shortly after Mrs. Baker's departure, was ill-advised. "To an early spring."

Mr. Wentworth drank to that. "I dread the hike back to Lynley Vale, and I consider myself as stout-hearted as the next man."

"You consort with Wentworths. You are more stout-hearted than most. What brings you to the village?"

Mr. Wentworth, whose daily business put him at the throbbing heart of international commerce and whose nearest associations were one step short of royalty, made a face as if he'd been served cold mashed turnips.

"Holiday shopping."

"Ah." Pietr joined Wentworth at the window, and indeed, fat, white snowflakes were drifting down from a pewter sky. Nothing to be alarmed about—yet. Mrs. Baker would reach York safely, though if the coachman were wise, he'd spend the night in town before asking the team to make the return journey.

"What am I supposed to give people who can buy entire counties if they so desire?" Mr. Wentworth asked.

Pietr handed out the same advice he gave to yeomen and gentry alike. "For the ladies, something small, unique, and pretty. For the gents, something comfortable and comforting. Avoid the useful and the necessary, which should be provided outside the context of holiday tokens. If you can make your gifts with your own hands, so much the better."

"I make deals," Mr. Wentworth said. "I make business transactions. I make coldly rational decisions."

This was the recitation of a man who'd never been in love. Of course Christmas would baffle him.

"We have a talented wood-carver in the person of Dody Wiles, who can usually be found holding forth in the inn's snug on a winter afternoon. For a price, he will make you birds, kittens, flowers... He can fashion them into coasters, or use a heavy wood such as mahogany to make a paperweight. His pipes are works of art, though he does require time to finish his creations."

"A wood-carver?"

"He was a drover who nearly lost a foot to frostbite. He needed a sedentary occupation, and the herds' loss is our gain. What on earth is that fellow thinking?"

A coach and four was careering along the far side of the village green, matched blacks in the traces.

"Fancy carriage," Mr. Wentworth muttered. "Fine horseflesh. What is a conveyance like that doing in a place like this?"

The vehicle rocked to a stop outside the coaching inn. A man climbed out. Youngish, based on the way he moved, dark-haired. He wore neither hat nor scarf nor gloves, though his greatcoat sported three capes.

He had no sooner put his booted foot to the snowy ground than he went careening onto his face into the nearest drift.

"Is this what passes for entertainment in a Yorkshire village?" Mr. Wentworth asked.

A lady climbed out of the coach. Her age was impossible to tell because she did wear a bonnet and scarf. She was spry, though, and she alit without benefit of a male hand to hold. She marched to her fallen comrade and stood over him, hands on hips.

He remained in the snow, facedown, unmoving.

"This is not entertainment," Pietr said, setting his drink aside. "This is a problem, and one I must deal with. The lady's coachy appears to be a madman and her escort three sheets to the wind. You are welcome to bide here, Mr. Wentworth, but I must pour oil on troubled waters and speak peace unto the heathen."

"You can't leave it to the innkeeper?"

"The hostlers aren't changing out the team, and our humble inn is full to the gills with holiday travelers. Yesterday's clouds promise that at some point today, the snow will mean business, and that woman will be stranded on the Dales with a drunk for an escort and an imbecile at the reins. Nobody will intervene now because she's not their problem, but I am a vicar and thus have a license to meddle."

Mr. Wentworth finished his drink and set the glass on the sideboard. "I have a propensity for meddling myself. Walden pays me to meddle, in fact. I didn't know there was a profession for it."

"Neither did I. You figure that part out after it's too late." Pietr did not bother with a hat, though he did tarry long enough to whip a scarf about his neck and pull on fleece-lined gloves. He stalked directly across the green, snow crunching beneath his boots, Mr. Wentworth tromping at his side.

By the time they reached the coach, so had the innkeeper, his wife, two aldermen, the blacksmith, Mrs. Peabody, and any number of guests from the inn.

"Mr. Sorenson, it's as well you've troubled yourself to join us." Mrs. Peabody managed to imply that Pietr had dawdled half the day away. As head of the pastoral committee, she took seriously her duty to ensure that her vicar walked *humbly* with his God. "Somebody is sorely in need of last rites."

"Looks to me," Mr. Wentworth said, "as if somebody needs a bit of hair of the dog."

Mrs. Peabody drew in a breath, like a seventy-four gunner unfurling her sails. "Sir, I don't know who you are, or why you feel—"

"Excuse me," Pietr said, bending over the prostrate man. "This fellow needs help. Mr. Wentworth, if you'd assist me to get him to his feet." Many a Yorkshire wayfarer had frozen to death while sleeping off the effects of drink in the cozy embrace of a fluffy snowdrift.

Pietr took one of the fellow's arms, Wentworth got the other, and they eased the man to his feet. He was flushed and bore the scent of spirits.

"What do you think you're doing with my brother?" The traveling companion's voice cracked like river ice giving way under a winter sun. What she lacked in stature she made up for in ire.

Jolly delightful. The situation needed only jugglers, a dancing bear, and a learned pig. Alas, Pietr would have to manage as best he could without those reinforcements.

As usual.

THE AIR WAS SO COLD, inhaling made the lungs shudder. Joy Danforth had not felt her feet for the past five miles, and she'd rejoiced at the sight of this snug little hamlet at the edge of the moor.

More fool her. The local welcoming committee had been ready to leave Hiram facedown in the snow. Then some hatless Viking, his coat flapping open, had stalked across the snowy green, probably intending to toss Hiram right back into the coach.

"Ma'am." The Viking managed a slight bow while holding Hiram up. "Pietr Sorenson, at your service. I have the happy privilege to be vicar in these surrounds, and I hope you will allow your brother to accept the hospitality of the manse. Our inn is full of holiday travelers, and your sibling needs shelter."

The tone of those words was so civilized, so erudite, that had Joy not been staring at the man, she would not know a bitter wind whipped the speaker's fair hair and turned his lean cheeks ruddy. A dark-haired fellow not quite as tall as the vicar had Hiram's other arm. That one had Bond Street written all over him, while the parson...

Impervious to the elements, slightly weathered, and as calm as a cathedral. Like one of those great edifices, he radiated substance—intellectual, physical, and moral substance—and Joy had little choice but to trust him. He was a vicar, albeit a more robust variety of vicar than Joy had encountered previously.

"I will accompany you," she said, though this provoked a mighty sniff from the broody hen with the atrocious bonnet.

"We will send over soup," the large woman on the steps said. "If the man is sick, he needs soup." She spared Hiram a baleful glance, came about like a frigate laden to the waterline, and disappeared into the inn.

"John," Joy called up to her coachman as the vicar and his companion started off with Hiram between them, "have my brother's valise sent along and get yourself something to eat."

The coachy nodded and signaled the team to plod forward.

Joy followed in the vicar's wake, keeping to the path already cut through the snow, and still the going was difficult. She nearly landed on her backside twice and silently cursed her lady's maid for insisting that Joy travel "in style." Style was silly little half boots. Style was only two lawn petticoats, lest the drape of embroidered skirts be disturbed. Style was no sturdy muff or proper scarf and only the thinnest of kid gloves.

"To blazes with style," Joy muttered as a frigid snowflake smacked her straight in the eye. "When I am Lady Apollo Bellingham, I will venture forth swaddled in old quilts if I please to."

By the time she stomped up the steps to the vicarage her ears were freezing, along with her nose, cheeks, and lips. The door opened, and the Viking motioned her inside.

"Please do come in, Miss Danforth. Mr. Wentworth is showing your brother to my study because the fire in the guest parlor hasn't been lit."

Mr. Sorenson exuded brisk hospitality and his sapphire-blue eyes conveyed genuine welcome, as if stranded travelers were all in a day's vicar-ing. Perhaps for him, they were.

"I apologize for imposing," Joy said through chattering teeth. "We won't stay long." She tried to pull off her gloves, but her fingers were too numb to get a proper grip on the leather. The ribbons of her bonnet were a more hopeless challenge, and even the buttons of her cloak joined the conspiracy to make her look clumsy and witless.

"Allow me," the vicar said, stepping close. "The cold is beastly, and we're only halfway through December. January looms in my nightmares, and February harbors my worst fears."

Warm fingers brushed Joy's chin, and a whiff of cedar tickled her nose. Then she was free of her bonnet. The vicar knew not to simply wrest her millinery away, for he took the trouble to remove Joy's hatpin first, lift the bonnet off carefully, and replace the hatpin in the crown.

He was apparently married, not that the future Lady Apollo Bellingham had any business noticing such a detail.

"Your gloves next?" he asked.

Joy surrendered to his assistance. "I can't recall when I've been this cold."

The vicar hung her bonnet and cloak on pegs. His greatcoat was draped on the next peg over, a garment more sturdy than fashionable. Even in the thin wintry light, Joy could tell that the house was spotless, and somebody—his wife?—had taken the time to hang mistletoe from the crossbeam and cloved oranges in the windows.

"Give me your hands," Mr. Sorenson said, holding out his own.

One obeyed vicars in the general case. Joy proffered hands red with cold. He enfolded them in a warm grasp and simply held her hands.

"No lap robes in that fancy coach of yours?"

"I used them for Hiram. He was shivering at one point, and then he wasn't, and then he was again. Might we go to him?" Though never had Joy appreciated what an animal comfort it could be simply to clasp hands. Perhaps life out near the moor fashioned that awareness, because the vicar seemed entirely comfortable with what in other surrounds would be an astonishing familiarity.

"Mr. Wentworth is with your brother," the vicar replied, letting go of Joy's hands. "We are without a housekeeper at present, but I have assisted in more sickrooms than you can imagine and am an adequate nurse. I don't suppose you're hungry?"

"I will be when I thaw out."

"Which might be about March?" He offered Joy a slight, conspiratorial smile as he led her down a corridor of polished oak flooring. The smile made him look impish. That such an otherwise austere countenance on such an imposing fellow could convey mischief came as a surprise.

Happily married, then.

Simple drawings were framed on the walls—a collie panting on a doorstep, a vase of painstakingly symmetric tulips, a butterfly on a blossoming branch. His children's work, no doubt, and a sweet touch for the vicarage's public areas. Joy thought back to her own fledgling efforts to make art and wondered what had become of her birds and bowls of fruit.

The study was a larger room than Joy had anticipated. Rather than a cramped lair full of books and newspapers and smelling of pipe smoke, the room might have more properly been called a library. The inside wall was lined with bookcases, while French doors and a pair of floor-to-ceiling windows let in the morning light. A chess set of ivory and ebony sat at a small table along the windows, the armies poised to begin battle.

A hearth occupied the third wall, and a blazing fire threw out both heat and the sharp tang of peat.

"Joy." Hiram croaked her name from a long sofa occupying the fourth wall. "I appear to be somewhat under the weather."

Mr. Wentworth draped a green and purple tartan blanket over Hiram's shoulders. "Ague would be my guess. Can come on quickly and knock a man on his—"

"Mr. Wentworth." The vicar spoke pleasantly. "A lady is present."

Mr. Wentworth grinned. "I do apologize. I meant to say that flu can knock a man sideways, particularly if a fellow has been dosing himself with an occasional nip. Do you have medicinals, Vicar, or shall I have some sent down from Lynley Vale?"

"A vicarage always has medical stores on hand. Mr. Danforth, how are you feeling?"

"About ninety years old and ready for a nap. I do apologize. Not the done thing to impose on strangers." He shivered and huddled into his blanket. "Should have dressed more warmly, I suppose."

Hiram should have left the brandy alone, at the very least. Joy would point that out to him when she and her brother had some privacy.

Mr. Sorenson knelt to pull off Hiram's boots. "I'm not sure clothing exists sufficient to take the teeth from a Yorkshire winter wind. Other foot."

"Are they ruined?" Hiram asked.

"Not nearly," Mr. Wentworth replied. "But they aren't very practical for this weather either. Hoby?"

Hiram nodded. "I treasure those boots. May never see their like again."

When I am Lady Apollo Bellingham, my brother will have new boots. Warm, practical, and stylish.

"Mr. Wentworth," the vicar said, "perhaps you could keep an eye out for our soup? The sooner we get our guests warm, the better. I will find some decent stockings for Mr. Danforth. Miss Danforth, do have a seat. The appointments are modest, but at your disposal. If you need to pen a note to somebody, the desk has writing supplies."

Joy sank into the seat behind a desk angled to take advantage of the natural light, though the chair dwarfed her. The vicar extracted another plaid blanket from a chest before the sofa and draped cedar-scented wool around Joy's shoulders.

"I'll be back in a moment. Please try not to fret, you two. Traveling in winter invariably meets with frustrations."

Then he was gone, leaving Joy swaddled in warmth and before a crackling fire, while her feet and fingers itched back to life.

"Sorry about this, Joy," Hiram said, patting his pockets and producing a flask. "Not much of an escort, am I?" He tipped the flask up, and shook a few drops into his mouth. "A vicarage. Whatever did I do to deserve the charity of a vicarage?"

He'd literally drunk himself into a snow drift. "You weren't given any choice." Mama and Papa had insisted that Hiram see Joy to the Bellingham family seat in person, because every opportunity for Hiram to gain the notice of his prospective brother-in-law must be exploited.

"Bedamned Yorkshire," Hiram said on a sigh. "You couldn't catch the eye of an earl's heir in Kent, could you? Had to be Yorkshire. I suppose it could be worse. Could have been some Hebridean chieftain whose heir took a fancy to you."

"Mama would have drawn the line at the Hebrides." Joy hoped. The Highlands were a fashionable walking destination, while the islands lacked social cachet.

Hiram's gaze landed on his once-beautiful, muddy, water-stained boots. "If that Hebridean chieftain had money, we'd be rowing out to his island at this moment. Bellingham must be sorely smitten with you, Joy."

"Need you sound so puzzled? I'm not awful."

Hiram's assessing gaze said she also wasn't the stuff a marquess's spare typically dreamed of, much less courted. "Treat your intended to that tone of voice, my girl, and he will row himself out to sea. Bellingham is quite a catch, and you are nearly at your last prayers. You know what Cunningham says."

Elvira Cunningham, Joy's erstwhile finishing governess, had aphorisms for every occasion. "The approach to spinsterhood," Joy quoted, "is like hacking out on a seasoned mount. The closer you come to your destination, the faster the journey goes. I am eight-and-twenty, Hiram. I do not need a finishing governess to explain my situation to me." Nine-and-twenty loomed just around the corner, in fact.

And a tired, nasty, honest part of Joy wanted to add that if Miss Cunningham had been as highly qualified as she'd believed herself to be, Joy's three London Seasons would have yielded matrimonial fruit rather than nothing more than aching feet, and a lot of bills from the milliners, modistes, and tailors.

"You need Apollo Bellingham's ring on your finger. Perhaps you could journey on without me?"

"Perhaps fever has rendered you delirious. Get well, and we'll be on our way. We can blame the delay on the weather, which is, indirectly, the truth."

Hiram looked like he wanted to argue—university had turned a sweet boy somewhat self-important—but the vicar returned, bearing a bundle of clothing and blankets.

"Until I have the fires going in the bedrooms, we'd best make you comfortable here, Mr. Danforth. This is my favorite room in the house. Small enough to be easily heated, and the view makes it peaceful too."

The view was a bleak expanse of snow, dotted with bare birches and aspens in the folds of the rolling countryside. An ancient manor peeked up from behind the nearest hill, and a walled orchard topped another.

"You don't find this view desolate?" Joy asked.

"Desolate?" Mr. Sorenson passed Hiram a pair of thick, knitted stockings. "My gracious, how could it be desolate? Open that window, and you'll hear the local children setting up a racket as they skate along the river. The orchard is sleeping now, but in a few months, the top of that hill will be literally awash in blooms. We have daffodils without number if you know where to look, and nothing in all of creation compares to the joy of watching spring lambs enjoy the fresh air."

As if to emphasize the vicar's words, a trio of robins fluttered onto a bird feeder set on a pole beyond the windows.

"You feed the birds?"

"The robins sing for us, even in winter. I am happy to reward their generosity."

Mr. Wentworth returned, bearing a wooden tray laden with a heavy crock swaddled in toweling. The vicar ladled out two bowls of steaming beef barley soup, laid a slab of generously buttered bread on the edge of each bowl, and reswaddled the crock.

"Enjoy," he said. "I'll see about getting the fires going in the bedrooms."

"We don't want to put you to any trouble," Joy said. "You have been more than kind." The scent of the soup was heavenly, and Hiram had already started in on his. No grace and no thanks for the food suggested he was feeling worse than he let on.

"To have some company on a chilly morning is my pleasure." The vicar bowed slightly and withdrew, and Mr. Wentworth followed in his wake.

"Will you write to Mama?" Hiram said, dunking his bread into the soup. "This feels good on my throat. Best eat it while it's hot, Joy."

Joy took a spoonful of hearty, tasty soup that had just the right amount of salt. "We should be on our way in another hour. I see no need to inform Mama of a slight delay. She would worry." And she would interrogate Joy.

Who is this Mr. Pietr Sorenson? Who are his people? Do we know *them?*

Which was Mama-ese for, *Do his people* have money?

At the moment, Joy did not particularly care who had money or who had titled relatives. Pietr Sorenson was kind and practical, and sometimes, that was worth more than all the money and titles in creation.

CHAPTER TWO

"I know how to light a coal fire," Ned Wentworth said, watching as Pietr used a lit taper to start the fire in the first guest bedroom. "I'm not familiar with the dirt you burn out here in the provinces."

"Peat is cheap, plentiful, and fragrant," Pietr replied, rising. "But we generally start a coal fire first and add the peat later." And in his opinion, if fire was wanted, then somehow, Ned Wentworth would figure out how to get one started. All the London tailoring in the world did not disguise how carefully he watched as Pietr stacked kindling over coals and a crumbly square of dried peat, then lit the kindling—early drafts of sermons—in three places.

"Miss Danforth has never lit a peat fire in her life," Ned said. "I can tell you that."

Though Ned Wentworth was only a few years older than Mr. Danforth, he apparently carried a great deal of responsibility and handled vast sums of money. Something about Ned worried Pietr, though, a subtle self-possession as vast and unyielding as the frigid moor.

Ned Wentworth was too young, and living too comfortable a life, to carry such coldness in his soul, but then, he was a Wentworth, whether he admitted it or not. Unfortunate experiences in earlier years had left their marks on that family.

"Miss Danforth is fashionably attired," Pietr said. "We don't see much fashion in the village, save for what our ducal neighbors display in the churchyard." Though neither the Wentworths nor the Roth-meres were prone to ostentation.

"Her brother should never have allowed her to set foot in that coach without a muff, scarf, hooded cloak, and decent boots. You will have two patients on your hands by nightfall. You could send them up to Lynley Vale."

The fire caught, and sparks crackled up the flue. The room would take hours to heat properly, but then the fieldstones of the old hearth would take in the warmth and radiate it out through the long, dark night.

"I am the vicar," Pietr said, a statement that had been a self-directed homily when he'd first come to this village. "Being a good Samaritan goes with the job, and if Mr. Danforth is contagious, he should stay put."

Wentworth ran a hand over a quilt folded at the foot of the bed, one Pietr's sister had sent along with him to Yorkshire all those years ago. The central theme was a pair of turtle doves wreathed in flowers and greenery.

What Clara lacked in subtlety, she made up for in exquisite needlework.

Wentworth left off smoothing the quilt. "One can be too virtuous, Sorenson. See that you don't come down with the ague yourself. I have the sense your little flock would soon fall to dicing and profanity if anything happened to you."

"Gracious heavens, not profanity. My holy ears would fall off. Dicing would give my blessed spleen palpitations."

"Your parishioners were ready to toss Danforth right back into his coach and consign him and his sister to the moors."

That bothered Wentworth, and bothered Pietr too. Time to preach about *entertaining angels unawares* again.

"Miss Danforth would have prevented that," Pietr said. She was small and sturdy, and despite her elegant attire, Pietr would have backed her in a fair verbal fight with Mrs. Blackwell any day. "Miss Danforth would have commanded a private dining room for the nonce and eventually shamed Blackwell into finding them a room. She is protective of her brother."

She should be in that private dining room, enjoying more impressive fare than bread and soup. Instead, she was in Pietr's study, probably wondering why a country vicar read salacious French novels and filthy Latin poetry.

"She'll expect you to wait on her," Wentworth replied, heading for the door. "What sort of woman dresses for Almack's when she's crossing the moor in December?"

"What sort of man comes to Yorkshire in December without knowing his way around a peat fire?"

Wentworth laughed as he reached the top of the steps. "Touché, Sorenson. Shall I take the dishes back to the inn for you?"

"Certainly not. Mrs. Blackwell will send her best spy, who will ask to sit for a bit in the kitchen to get warm—it being approximately fourteen miles across the green—and the lad will carry a detailed report back to his commanding officer."

"They watch you that closely? I would not enjoy that."

"You watch the Wentworths that closely. When one cares, one pays attention." Would Pietr's successor take that approach to leading the village flock? Or would the bishop send out some old relic who bleated on about damnation and fallenness? The congregation would lap up that sort of scold, as they seldom did Pietr's little maunderings on loving thy neighbor and casting out the beam from thine own eye first.

His Grace of Rothhaven had authority over the vicarage's living, and he would not suffer a fool or a windbag to take Pietr's place. Nor would *Her* Grace, for that matter.

"I'd best pay attention to my errands," Wentworth said when they'd reached the bottom of the steps. "I will report that the patient is resting comfortably and expected to make a full recovery."

Pietr held his coat for him, then passed him hat, gloves, and scarf. "You will want to be expeditious about your errands, Mr. Wentworth. The snow is merely flirting with us now, but by this afternoon, we could well be in the midst of serious weather."

Wentworth peered out the window beside the door. "How can you tell?"

A feeling in the bones, which were not exactly young bones anymore. "We can see the sky here, unlike your situation in London once the coal fires start roaring. We can see the clouds, feel the wind. Yesterday, we had the sort of high, wispy mares' tail clouds that make for a spectacular sunset. This morning we rose to more of a quilted sky, and that presages greater mischief. Don't dawdle in the village, no matter how much you dread returning to Lynley Vale."

Mr. Wentworth buttoned up and tossed his scarf around his shoulders. "I don't dread it so much as I feel as if I'm visiting a foreign country full of addled citizens. Holiday decorations, singing footmen, mistletoe dangling from every chandelier. No restraint whatsoever. The duke is the worst of the lot, calling the children elves and making up silly lyrics for the carols."

"How dreadful," Pietr said, redraping Mr. Wentworth's scarf so it would provide some protection for his ears and chin. "Be wary, sir, lest the high spirits take you captive. Next thing you know, you will join in for a chorus or two of 'Good King When Does This Song Ever End,' and civilization will cease to exist. Stand firm against the temptation to holiday merriment, Mr. Wentworth. The curmudgeons of rural Yorkshire are counting on you."

"The duke calls it that—'Good King When Does This Song Ever End.'"

"Where do you think he heard it first?" Pietr lifted the door latch. "On your way, and be mindful of Blackwell's winter ale. The stuff is brewed for Yorkshiremen—and for our womenfolk."

Mr. Wentworth departed on a gust of stinging cold air. Pietr said a quick prayer of the secular sort that Ned would find his way safely back to Lynley Vale, but then, Ned Wentworth had the air of a man who'd weathered many storms.

He'd find his way to the manor. Finding his way home would be a more complicated matter.

"Do you always tuck up your guests as if they were small boys come to study with you and send them off smiling?" Joy Danforth leaned against the doorway to the unused guest parlor.

She was not smiling. Her hems were damp, she clutched the blanket about her like an oversized shawl, and her coiffure, which should have been a sensible chignon, but had probably started out as an *artful creation*, had turned into bedraggled masses of damp curls.

"Mr. Wentworth is a banker. Merriment inspired by a particular date on the calendar unnerves him."

"Merriment unnerves a lot of people." She pushed away from the doorjamb and turned a pensive gaze on the white expanse beyond the window. "I heard what you said about the weather. Hiram and I should be on our way."

Yes, they should, though it occurred to Pietr he had no idea where they might be going or why they must hurry off.

"The inns farther west are humble and few, Miss Danforth, and your brother is unwell. What compels you to travel on?"

She rested her forehead against the pane of glass. "Utter necessity, of course. I am to spend the holidays with the Bellingham family near Hambleton. Do you know them?"

Pietr knew *of* them, as did everybody in the northern counties. "Your coachman missed the turn, if your destination was Hambleton, and in this weather, you're a good two days of frigid travel from your destination."

"*Two days?*" Her tone suggested he might as well have said two years. "I told Hiram we should have been heading west, not south. He did not listen to me."

A vicarage without a housekeeper had loomed like a promised

land of solitude, a chance to mentally say farewell to years of good work among good people. A relief beyond description.

Though a bit lonely, truth be told. A bit tedious.

"Stay here for now," Pietr said, though he hadn't planned on issuing quite that invitation. "You are safe and warm. I am on hand to assist with your brother if his illness worsens, and the Bellingham family seat hasn't moved for four hundred years. Stay."

Miss Danforth stood straight, faint humor touching her gaze. "Four hundred and sixty-seven years. I want to argue with you, but you are right: I am warm and safe. Hiram will listen to you, though he no longer pays any mind to me, and we are not expected on a date certain. I should tell my coachman we'll bide here for a night."

"We will send word with Mrs. Blackwell's potboy when he comes to retrieve the soup bowls, and Mr. Blackwell will give your coachy a bunk with the grooms and hostlers. Our innkeeper is not as uncharitable as he may appear. We get the occasional fashionable lord passing through on the way to the grouse moors. Such young men can be troublesome even when not inebriated."

Miss Danforth muttered something that sounded like *can they ever*. "I will need my valise."

"I am happy to fetch it for you. First, may I presume to lend you a pair of my knitted stockings? My sister makes them. Our mama was Danish, and Clara's stockings are the equal of any winter chill."

This disclosure occasioned a full-on, where-has-that-been-hiding? smile from Miss Danforth. "Your mother is a Dane?"

"Was. I get my height from her side of the family, I'm told. This amuses you?"

Her smile softened. "I'm pleased, Mr. Sorenson. I'm pleased."

Mr. Danforth called out from the study, and the smile faded like a winter night enveloping a sunset.

"I'd best go to him," Miss Danforth said. "Thank you again for your hospitality."

"My pleasure. You'll find my stockings in the top drawer of the bureau in the first bedroom on the right upstairs. I'll fetch your bags."

"My thanks." Miss Danforth climbed the steps with all the dignity of a monarch in her robes of state, while Pietr bundled up and prepared for a little jaunt over to the inn. Cold air was supposedly good for clearing a man's head, which was abruptly a muddled place indeed.

Joy Danforth had fashionable connections and traveled in even more fashionable style. Why, then, was she utterly unconcerned about the state of her hair? Why were her fingers ink-stained, as if she pored over ledgers and correspondence by the hour? Why were the nails of her left hand bitten down, while those of the right were neatly manicured?

Paying attention to a guest wasn't the same thing as being nosy, though Pietr did admit to some curiosity. A little curiosity, anyway.

A MAN with a wife would have offered Joy the loan of a pair of stockings belonging to the lady of the house. That realization struck as Joy entered the first bedroom on the right at the top of the steps. She went to the window, which had a view of the green and of the undulating hills beyond the village.

The vicar made his way across the open space at the brisk pace of a man made fit by regular exertion. He respected the elements, and Joy had the fanciful notion that they—the wind, sky, and hills—respected him too.

Why no wife for such an estimable gentleman? Not that it was any of Joy's business.

Mr. Sorenson disappeared into the inn, and rather than stand watch until he reemerged, Joy surveyed his private quarters. Her first impression was of tidiness. The hearth was swept, the four-poster bed neatly made. No vanity, but the top of the bureau held a folding mirror, and the comb, brush, scent bottle, and stack of handkerchiefs were precisely arranged before it.

She peeked behind the privacy screen to find more order and

organization. A shaving kit, basin, and pitcher occupied a washstand. A stitched sampler hung from the privacy screen. Joy expected to find the Twenty-third Psalm, but instead, somebody had memorialized Ephesians 4:26. *Be ye angry, and sin not. Let not the sun go down upon your wrath.*

Interesting choice.

The bedside table told another interesting tale. Mr. Sorenson read poetry, as well as both a York and a London newspaper. One bound book was clearly in a Scandinavian tongue, another—*Tales of an Unhappy Wife*—in French. One of Mrs. Radcliffe's novels was tucked between them.

A restless and voracious mind lurked amid all this tidiness. A Viking mind, roaming the literary world in search of intellectual plunder.

Joy was tempted to inspect the dressing closet and look under the bed, but Hiram called out again from below. Besides, the vicar had given her permission to peek into his bedroom, not pry into his life.

The bureau was another testament to organization, the stockings rolled and tucked neatly in rows in the top drawer, which was nearly at Joy's eye level. The drawers were cedar lined, a small extravagance, but probably necessary when a wardrobe depended so heavily on wool.

"Joy! Are you coming?"

She hurried off, taking care to leave the door open so some of the warmth from the lower floor would reach the bedroom.

"What on earth is amiss, Hiram?" she asked, descending the steps.

"I need a headache powder."

He was slightly flushed, and his eyes had a sheen to them that Joy associated with genuine illness. Even so, Hiram was a grown man, having officially reached his majority. This rudeness was tiresome.

"When Mr. Sorenson comes back with our valises, I will ask him to prepare you a powder. He said the vicarage is well stocked with medicinals."

Hiram made a face. "D'you suppose there's a chamber pot somewhere nearby?"

"Hiram Danforth, I am not your nanny. It's as if you grew younger at university instead of more mature."

"You are no help."

"Try a guest bedroom upstairs. Look for a room with a fresh fire."

Hiram disappeared up the steps, his tread heavy. When had he become so uncharming? Half of Mama's argument for a match between Joy and Lord Apollo was to ensure that Hiram made the right connections and enjoyed the right opportunities.

The other half... Joy did not want to think about the other half.

She returned to the cozy study and swapped her sodden stockings for the luxurious comfort of the vicar's wool. A lady did not go about unshod, but so substantial were Mr. Sorenson's knitted stockings that Joy hardly needed slippers.

She was folding up the blanket Hiram had discarded on the sofa, idly watching the birds at the feeder, when she caught sight of her reflection in the window.

"Heaven defend me." A Medusa stared back at her, hair spiraling madly, curls bouncing halfway down her back, wisps and ringlets framing her face. "I look like a startled hedgehog."

"So you do," Hiram said, coming through the doorway, "but at least you ain't sick. I feel more wretched by the hour."

"Hiram, why didn't you tell me my coiffure was in want of repair?" The *vicar* had seen her thus. Mr. Wentworth had seen her... Thank heavens she hadn't arrived at the Bellingham estate in such a condition.

"Your coiffure often wants repair. I'd lend you my comb, except that would be like aiming a peashooter at the French army. Other girls wear fashionably short curls, but my sister must resemble the Renaissance saints in their spiritual agonies. God, I feel miserable." He sank onto the couch. "I don't think that soup agreed with me."

"How much have you had to drink, Hiram?" He'd begun the

journey from York up on the box with the coachman, and Joy suspected he'd refilled his flasks at the inn.

"Not enough, clearly. Give me back my blanket. I've a mind to catch a few winks." He unceremoniously stretched out on the couch, jammed a pillow behind his head, and rolled to face the wall. "Blighted Yorkshire. This is all your fault."

Joy draped the blanket over him. "Go to sleep. Rest can only help."

A note to Mama was required if they were to spend the night at the vicarage, but first Joy would do something about her hair. She took the seat near the hearth, tucked her feet up under her, and began fishing pins from the wreckage.

She'd have to manage without a comb or brush, though she still knew how to fashion a braid and secure it with pins into a coronet.

When I am Lady Apollo Bellingham, I will wear my hair in braids if I wish. I will have warm stockings. I will read whatever I please to read. She had embellished considerably on that comforting mental litany by the time her hair was completely undone.

Hiram snored on the couch, the birds had left the feeder, and the only sound was the crackling of the fire. Joy should thus have heard the front door open, but she was too engrossed in the speculative pleasures of marriage to Lord Apollo.

She was taken completely unaware when the study door opened to reveal the vicar, hair damp, cheeks ruddy, standing in the doorway and frankly staring at her.

"I LOOK A FRIGHT," Miss Danforth said. "I do apologize."

Pietr moved into the study and closed the door behind him. "Then I must look a fright as well, for I, too, have been at winter's mercy."

Miss Danforth blushed, and never had a fright looked so... so... fetching. So arrestingly feminine. Of all the possibilities Pietr could have conjured when he'd opened his study door, a dark-haired pixie perched in his reading chair had not been among them.

And behind that purely male reaction was a widower's appreciation for the female in her domestic state. Watching a woman take down her hair was a husband's intimate privilege—or a lover's—and one Pietr had failed to appreciate when it had been his. Unbound hair was a metaphor for relaxation of both moral and emotional guard, something a lady would allow only if she felt safe.

"I've brought your valises," Pietr said. "You doubtless have a comb and brush among your effects, and you must not stand on ceremony. This is the only truly warm room in the house, other than the kitchen, and I was frequently tasked with brushing out my wife's hair of an evening."

Miss Danforth let a half-finished braid unravel. "You were married?"

"Briefly. Long ago." Shockingly long ago, upon reflection. "Mr. Danforth is asleep?"

"I suspect in addition to illness, he is suffering the results of excessive attempts to medicate himself."

"Or," Pietr said, regarding the prone form on his sofa, "did the medication induce the illness? Brandy doesn't create real warmth, only disregard for the cold. A couple of years back, a post coach got stranded on the moor in a winter storm. The horses froze to death, as did the coachy and guard. The men had no less than six empty flasks between them, and there's no telling how often those flasks had been refilled throughout the day."

"And had they been sober, would those men have chanced the moor?" Miss Danforth murmured. "A cautionary tale indeed." She twiddled the end of a dark ringlet around her finger. "I know why you didn't say anything about my hair. You are a gentleman, and if a lady is in complete disarray, you will pretend to ignore the problem."

"You were not in complete disarray, Miss Danforth. You were merely a trifle discommoded by travel."

She sent him a peevish look that he found utterly enchanting.

Nobody was peevish with the vicar, though they had ample reason to be.

"You need not flatter me, sir. You were being considerate. Hiram should have said something, but Hiram no longer sees me as... He doesn't see me at all."

"Hiram is your brother." Pietr crossed the room to toss another square of peat onto the fire. "In his way, he is doubtless endearing— also exquisitely vexatious. I have a sister, you will recall, and Clara is determined that I take my place in the world. I thought *here* was my place, but siblings have the ear of God, according to Clara. Thus I am off to become assistant dean of a cathedral forty miles distant. From there, to dean, and—Clara is short for clairvoyant—I will have my own episcopal see before I'm fifty, as if the Church is a cricket team, and I can aspire to captain's honors."

"You have no wish to become a bishop."

"What makes you say that?" Pietr was supposed to have those aspirations, just as he'd been supposed to remarry the perfect wife of Clara's choosing. Of course, he'd also been supposed to aspire to a diplomatic post, but—given the state of matters on the Continent until recently—Papa had permitted ordination instead.

A fallback measure, he'd said, until the armies go home, which British armies never seemed to do for long.

"I perceive nothing about you that smacks of worldly ambition," Miss Danforth said. "You feed the birds. You grasp why the Black-wells are leery of inebriated young men in London finery. You tuck Mr. Wentworth's scarf about his ears."

What was she going on about? "One tries to be useful."

The finger twiddling the lock of hair stilled. "Has your bishop been useful to you?"

What a peculiar question. "I make an annual sojourn into York to confer with him. I used to go quarterly, then semiannually. Now I drop a regular note and take tea with him once a year. He does not meddle with me, and that is a significant form of usefulness."

"He does not *see* you," Miss Danforth said, rising. "Hiram does not see me, but, Mr. Sorenson, I did appropriate a pair of your stockings, and marvelous stockings they are too." She took one of the chairs at the chess table and arranged her blanket about her legs.

She had taken off her boots and wore only the thick, cream wool stockings Clara sent yearly by the dozen. Those stockings would come well past Miss Danforth's knees, an image Pietr ought not to be imagining.

"You have a mirror over your vanity," Miss Danforth went on. "I noticed this, and I noticed how tidily your effects are maintained. I noticed the simplicity of that room—no art on the walls, no fussy little curios, and no theological tomes displayed for vanity's sake. You like your comforts—fluffy pillows, thick quilts and rugs, plenty to read—but you are no hedonist."

"Are we to have a game of chess, Miss Danforth?"

"I feel compelled to keep an eye on Hiram, and I haven't had a good game in ages."

"Nor have I. My best partner became preoccupied with wedded bliss. Lord Nathaniel's infrequent games haven't been the same since." Pietr took the second chair. "What else did you notice about my living quarters?"

He turned the board, giving his guest white, so she had the tactical advantage of the first move. "It's what I did not notice that matters. I was frankly curious about mine host's private quarters, but, Mr. Sorenson, I stood directly in front of your bureau, and I did not see my own reflection in your folding mirror. I look like I've survived a North Sea gale, and I did not see *myself*."

While Miss Danforth studied the board, Pietr studied her. He could make some pious little observation about humility being a virtue and vanity unattractive, but Miss Danforth was probing a troubling issue.

"You've lapsed into taking tea with yourself annually?"

She nodded. "If that. When and why did I lose sight of myself? I must think on this. When do you leave for your deanship?"

"Too soon, though I haven't said anything to the parishioners yet.

They will all want to have me to dinner, when I prefer to slip quietly into a passing coach." The more pressing question was not when he'd leave for a deanship, but why. Clara had conveniently supplied him with the answer in many a letter: *to better serve the Church*, which was how Clara alluded to escaping the Dales.

"Your move, Miss Danforth, and I warn you, I will allow no gentlemanly sensibilities to spare you defeat."

"Nor will ladylike sensibilities on my part preserve you from an ignominious fate, Mr. Sorenson. Prepare to defend yourself."

The words rang with layered meanings, though Miss Danforth could not know that, and still, Pietr lost the first game.

CHAPTER THREE

The vicar's chess was refreshingly ruthless.

Joy had lost two pawns to his one before she got into the spirit of the contest, old skills creaking and stretching to life as if coming out of hibernation. He was a think-once-think-twice-and-move sort of player, given to direct attacks and plenty of them.

"We are an interesting contrast in styles," she said when his king lay prone on the board. "You dispatch your strategies with single-minded purpose, while I dither and look for a way through the postern gate."

His smile was slightly puzzled. "I'd say you rather took my postern gate off its hinges. Another game?"

"Of course." Joy passed him the white king. "I played against my grandfather when I was a girl. I was the only child for years before Hiram came along, and Grandpapa made do with me as best he could."

"Is your grandfather still among the living?"

"Alas, no. He went to his reward just as I was to make my come out, which meant I did not make my come out as scheduled." Joy set up the black army, her preferred color. Better to lie in wait for the foe than to strike the first blow. "The litany of disasters since then is long and boring." Mostly, that litany was expensive. Hopelessly, stupidly expensive.

"And yet, I see no evidence of disaster. I see a worthy opponent, who is about to be taught a lesson in locked postern gates."

The second game absorbed Joy in a way she hadn't felt since Grandpapa's final illness. She and he had played for hours then, for she'd sensed that on the chessboard, Grandpapa was still hale and whole. In the person of his knights and rooks, he'd been nimble, powerful, and wily.

She lost track of time, she lost track of her queen's rook, and she lost track of Hiram snoring on the couch. Her world came down to besting her opponent, though she had to content herself with a draw.

"My honor is not quite restored," Mr. Sorenson said, "but my pride is slightly recovered. You truly are formidable, Miss Danforth."

"I had forgotten the exhilaration of a good game. I should never have lost that rook."

"I should have captured both of your rooks and your queen. Too busy guarding my postern gate, I suppose. Tell me of the disasters."

Losing a rook was hardly... "Oh, those disasters. They make a boring recitation."

The vicar picked up her queen and returned the lady to her home square. "Not as boring as working on my next sermon. Besides, I told you I was leaving for a deanship, and thus we have become confidants."

To be this man's confidant was no small thing. "When will you tell your congregation?"

His gaze went to the bird feeder, devoid of winged visitors. "The first Sunday of the new year, I suppose. My replacement should be on his way here by then. Weather permitting, I will be off to my new post shortly thereafter."

"Do you want the weather to permit?"

"Yes. I have tarried here on the moor long enough, and I'm not getting any younger. Tell me of your disasters."

During the chess match, the day had shifted from morning to afternoon. This far north, at this time of year, sunset came before four p.m., and given the overcast sky, afternoon had already taken on the quiet feel of a long, quiet evening.

"I should not complain," Joy said. "My prospects are very encouraging, and I am in many ways the luckiest of women."

Mr. Sorenson tossed a pawn into the air and caught it. "I hear a but lurking in the undergrowth, Miss Danforth, or several buts."

"But fashions change from one season to the next, so my entire wardrobe had to be replaced. Without Grandpapa to manage the finances, Papa has not prospered." No self-respecting Danforth admitted that Grandpapa's expertise had been the font of family coin, for that shaded perilously close to acknowledging a connection to *trade*.

"Many families have seen their fortunes decline," Mr. Sorenson said. "With the war, with the peace, with a bad harvest. Fifty years ago, the Danish and English royal houses intermarried. Less than twenty years ago, we were at war with the Danes, sacking their capital, and now we're all great good friends again. My family's situation has been challenging, what with cousins and grandparents in both Denmark and England. I do hope your family's difficulties will resolve themselves."

He had not asked a question, precisely, but rather, issued an invitation, and where was the harm in airing family linen to a rural vicar?

"Seasons are expensive," Joy said, arranging pieces on their home squares. "I did not *take*. I am not willowy. I am not blond. I have no airs and graces. I read excessively. I play chess."

"You play chess quite well."

The vicar sat across from Joy, a man very much at ease in his body. At some point, he'd turned back the cuffs of his sleeves and shed his jacket, for the fire threw out a good heat. When a lady's hair was cascading down her back, and her brother snored away the afternoon on the sofa, strict propriety could also take a nap.

"To play chess well is a singular failing in an unmarried lady, Mr.

Sorenson. I had to learn that. I had to learn how to toss a game without seeming to. Lord Apollo can barely keep straight how the pieces move, and yet, I must allow him to best me."

"I can't say this Lord Apollo impresses me very much. He should either ask you for instruction or take his lumps like a gentleman."

"Ask *me* for instruction? You have not moved much in London Society, have you?"

He rose and stretched, then poked at the fire and added more fuel. "I met my wife in London. Papa was a baronet, Clara an heiress of modest proportions, thanks to Grandmama. I was the handy second son dragged along to every *soirée*, ball, and ridotto in the Home Counties. My wife rescued me from all that, though she would say I did the rescuing."

"You miss her."

Mr. Sorenson set aside the poker and rearranged the blanket over Hiram's prone form. "We were not married long enough for resentments and annoyances to take the shine off of our affections. We were still infatuated, still gleefully rejoicing to have taken the step into adulthood that confers a sort of freedom even while it also creates constraints. We saw only the freedoms and availed ourselves of them liberally."

He referred at least in part to marital intimacy, though perhaps he alluded to more subtle pleasures. Joy could not imagine what those pleasures would be, and with Lord Apollo, the intimacies loomed like a particularly awkward quadrille to be endured. His lordship was prone to chattering, though being a lordship, the received description was that he was an excellent conversationalist.

"Why haven't you remarried, Mr. Sorenson?"

He set up the white army, piece by piece, without resuming his seat. "At first, I was grieving. Merry young wives are not to be carried off by lung fever. God and I had many a discussion on that topic. Then I was busy finding my footing with the Church. Then I was besieged by the local ladies, and I could not choose one from among them for fear of dashing the hopes of the others. By virtue of tireless good manners, unrelenting small talk, and a complete lack of dash, I have become the harmless widower who can be relied upon to make up the numbers."

His chess painted a very different picture—no small talk and plenty of dash.

"Isn't a dean typically married?"

He sent her a bleak smile and regarded the lengthening shadows in the snowy yard. "I am not a dean yet, and you have completely thwarted my polite inquiries as to your own circumstances. What has sent you careening across the moors in the dead of winter, Miss Danforth? I suspect you are overdue to entrust the tale to somebody, and it appears we are to be cast upon one another's company for some time."

He beckoned Joy from her chair, though it took some rearranging of her blanket-cum-shawl for her to get to her feet. She joined him at the window and saw to her amazement that the pole supporting the bird feeder had become buried a good six inches deeper in snow.

"That sky," he said, pointing to a bank of billowing, dark gray clouds tinged with pink on the bottom, "presages more snow. A lot more. I am very glad you did not attempt to travel on, Miss Danforth. Very glad indeed."

Joy was tempted to slip an arm around his waist and rest against him. She and Hiram could well have been stuck in some drift, bickering their way to a cold death. They might have been stranded in surrounds far less commodious than this tidy vicarage. They might have both taken ill and been consigned to sickness or worse on the moor.

"I am glad too, Mr. Sorenson."

"Call me Pietr," he said. "You have breached my postern gate, after all, and you are about to tell me your troubles."

"Am I?"

"Yes, but for such a momentous undertaking, we ought to brew up a pot of tea, don't you think? Hiram remains clasped in the arms of Morpheus—probably the best thing for him—while I must make sure the fire in the kitchen does not go out. Borrow my slippers, and we'll soon have the kettle on."

What had begun as an inconvenient and short detour was rapidly taking on the contours of an adventure. Joy spared Hiram one look—snoring away, indeed—and slid her feet into a pair of large slippers that had sat warming on the hearth.

"A pot of tea sounds like just the thing, Vicar, but my troubles are hardly momentous."

"I will be the judge of that. Come along, and I will show you the sort of temptation I face when my housekeeper departs on a winter holiday."

He held out a hand, and his gaze portended mischief. Harmless mischief, which was probably how the very worst mischief presented itself.

The prudent move would be to demur and cite a need to decently arrange hair now thoroughly dry. A proper young lady would allude to having to unpack her valise—a ten-minute exercise at best—and leave the vicar to his temptations.

Joy put her hand in his and followed him down to the kitchen.

"THE BISHOP HAS SENT me another round of candidates to consider." Robert, His Grace of Rothhaven, passed his brother an epistle written in the exquisite hand of an ecclesiastical scribe. "We may have our choice of two naughty boys who barely avoided scandal as curates or three doddering tipplers. My immortal soul is not impressed."

Nathaniel's calls on the family seat were less frequent these days, in part because Robert himself ventured over to Lynley Vale on occasion. The first time he'd walked alone from one estate to the other, a distance of less than a mile, he'd felt as if he'd conquered a vast wilderness and returned victorious from the wars.

An epileptic duke took his sense of accomplishment where he

could find it. Pietr Sorenson had come across Robert making that sojourn and simply wished him a pleasant ramble.

No hovering, no inquisition, no peeking about in hopes of spotting a footman-nanny. "Enjoy the lovely day, Your Grace," said with that smile Sorenson had that intimated vast delight in all of creation.

Nathaniel frowned at the list of names and their descriptors. "This is the third such team of reprobates the right reverend bishop has sent you. We might be a small congregation of unimaginative sinners, but we pay our tithes. We deserve a proper haranguing once a week."

Nathaniel ought to be getting back to Lynley Vale, for the snow had not let up, and darkness approached. How lovely to be the brother doing the fretting for a change. And to be doing normal, fraternal fretting, about the predictably disobliging Yorkshire weather.

Sorenson had made that point to Robert: That to have petty annoyances to complain about, rather than soul-destroying fears and grievances, was something to be grateful for. In typical Pietr Sorenson fashion, he'd not harangued. He'd simply remarked that he himself was the most fortunate of men, for his worst tribulations included nothing more vexing than listening to Biddy Peabody's imaginary ailments or teaching a fresh crop of children to skate each year.

The scold to a wealthy peer enjoying general good health and a happy marriage had been so subtle as to be barely perceptible, though Robert doubted that such burdens were Sorenson's worst tribulations. A handsome, intelligent, supremely agreeable widower who eschewed remarriage was no stranger to loneliness.

"Do you suppose the bishop is trying to tell us something?" Nathaniel asked, passing back the letter. The cribbage board sat on the table between them. The play had been dull, but then, the play was for old times' sake, no longer a weapon to be wielded against the demons of boredom on a bitter Yorkshire night.

"The bishop is suggesting I convince Sorenson to stay?"

"We've had curates by the dozen," Nathaniel replied. "They never last. They endure about two years by the moor, two years in which they are frequently off to visit aging relatives or spinster sisters, and then they're gone. Durham, the Midlands, anywhere but our village. Two ducal residences in the neighborhood is probably what draws such fellows, but they lack Sorenson's calling."

Robert folded up the bishop's epistle to the heathen on the moor. Robert would consult with his duchess, who would help him fashion a reply: *We need a vicar who cares about us. Who has a sense of humor and a sense of discretion. A man who can use Scripture to comfort far more often than he does to exhort. A fellow who doesn't bat an eye at finding a half-mad duke lurking among his congregants.*

"Sorenson has humility," Robert said. "Genuine consideration for others. What does it say about us, Nathaniel, that we could return to our reclusive ways, the Wentworths could decide to once again leave Lynley Vale to factors and stewards, and the parishioners would barely notice? Take Sorenson away, and twenty years on, they will still fondly recall the old vicar."

"He's not old," Nathaniel said, rising. "By church standards, he's served out his terms and is ready for the first in a series of brilliant promotions. If we value him, and we do, we must not stand in his way."

Robert got to his feet as well. "I am the last person to confine another in uncongenial surrounds—to confine another anywhere—but Sorenson understands this place, Nathaniel. He understands the people, and even the livestock, weather, and wildlife. Promotion is all very well, but would Sorenson decline a summons from the Church if he knew he was appreciated here?"

"He knows we love him," Nathaniel said, "and I use that word advisedly. He has never violated a confidence, never turned me aside no matter how bad my chess. He was the closest thing to a friend Althea had, and he has the knack of judging the annual Fair Day baking contest such that the losers are flattered as thoroughly as the winners."

"And that matters," Robert said, ushering Nathaniel from the warmth of the family parlor. "Constance would say that diplomacy regarding the ladies' pies is part of the reason why this village has no mendicants or inebriates."

"Althea and Constance have something to do with that," Nathaniel said, peering out the window in the foyer. "Looks like we're in for it tonight."

Robert held his brother's greatcoat for him. "Good snuggling weather."

Nathaniel grinned. "It's all good snuggling weather in Yorkshire, and Althea has stripped half the trees on the estate of their mistletoe. Morale at Lynley Vale is good of late."

"Morale at Rothhaven Hall is... Something of a holiday bacchanal is already under way, though the riot subsides when I walk into a room. Constance abets the staff, goes about humming carols and ordering Cook to test different recipes for wassail."

"About time the old place saw some yuletide mischief." Nathaniel pulled on his gloves and wrapped a thick scarf about his chin and ears. "Loki will delight in the new snow."

"Loki had best not put a foot wrong, or we'll be dining on horse-meat at Christmas."

"He loves this weather, and he's finally settling down. Typical Rothmere, late to mature, but a good soul at heart."

Nathaniel whacked Robert on the shoulder, and then he was off into the frigid, gathering gloom. Robert stood for a moment on the terrace, watching his brother swing into the saddle and trot off down the lane.

By decree of the ladies, paths were kept shoveled from the house to the stable, from Rothhaven Hall's garden to Lynley Vale's park and from the park up to the manor house. Benches along those paths were regularly swept free of snow, and no disobliging boulder or protruding rock was permitted near the trails.

Robert was not to suffer a seizure and die wandering out on the moor. He was to keep to the safe paths. Because he had much to live for, he did exactly that—except when abed with his duchess, at which times, wild behavior abounded.

Nathaniel's great beast of a horse preferred the challenge of the elements and thus went frisking and capering down the drive, leaving the profound quiet of deep winter in his wake.

In the village, Pietr Sorenson dwelled alone in his vicarage, as he had been dwelling for years. Had he asked for the notice of his church superiors? Did he *want* to leave? Was it the greater kindness to let him go or to insist that he stay, for if any man was deserving of kindness, Sorenson was that fellow.

And yet, in all the years Sorenson had shepherded the local flock, he'd maintained a certain subtle reserve. The last citadel of a man's dignity was the privacy of his thoughts and feelings. One did not intrude on such preserves lightly. With Pietr Sorenson, Robert wasn't sure one even could, his parapets were that well defended.

～

"THIS IS THE MEDICINAL PANTRY," Mr. Sorenson said. "Mrs. Peabody keeps us well supplied."

He opened what looked like a made-over wardrobe, one that had been fitted with shelves, drawers, and interior cabinets. The workmanship was exquisite, the knobs all carved to resemble tiny birds in flight.

"Mrs. Peabody was the woman who wanted Hiram to have last rites?" A beady-eyed little creature who would have looked to have misplaced her cauldron and pointed hat.

"She means well," Mr. Sorenson said. "Mrs. Peabody was one of seven daughters, and only she and one sibling remain. None of the ladies married advantageously. All were widowed young, and thus penury is a constant worry for Biddy and her sister. They sell their tisanes, some of which are surprisingly effective, but mostly, they worry about which of them will go next."

Abruptly, Joy was ashamed. "That is awful. Nobody should sit around waiting for death to roll the dice." An unwelcome thought intruded: Why sit around waiting for Lord Apollo Bellingham to propose?

Though he would. Joy was nearly certain of it.

The vicar brushed his fingers over the burnished wooden wing of a hawk. "We think of the elderly as peacefully rocking away the years, and perhaps that's true for a few of them, but I suspect the reality for many requires more courage than they ever had to call upon earlier in life."

He began opening drawers and cupboards. "Here we have the tonics and tisanes, the purges—Mrs. Peabody's purges are the equal of any you will find in Harrogate—and the elixirs to prevent baldness. My own copious locks owe their location on my head solely to Mrs. Peabody's good offices, as she will doubtless tell you twice at every assembly."

"I like your locks." Joy also liked having her own hair for once unconfined during daylight hours, though she really ought to braid it up.

"I like hearing Mrs. Peabody brag." Mr. Sorenson closed up the cupboards and drawers. "She pets my hair as if I'm her prize hound. You must not tell a soul, but I have never been able to bring myself to use her elixir. Smells of rotten fish. The cats lap it up like coachmen doing justice to the summer ale."

"The cats?"

The vicar moved along the passage to a back door. Darkness would soon descend, and the path out to what looked like a stable, chicken coop, and garden shed combined was blanketed in new snow.

He opened the door. "Here, kitty, kitty, kitty! Come along, you louts. Supper awaits."

The cold was a physical force pushing into the passage, though the fresh air was also invigorating.

The vicar cupped his hands around his mouth. "I said *come along!*"

Two dark shapes wiggled through a low gap in the boards of the stable and came up the drifted path in a series of bounds. A pair of enormous felines shook the snow from their luxurious fur and strolled into the hallway, tails high, as if they'd just handed their vouchers to a footman at Almack's.

"I have never seen such grand specimens," Joy said. "They look impervious to the elements." They resembled miniature lynxes, with tufted ears and poufy feet. One was a flaming ginger with yellow eyes and a white bib, the other a splendid blend of tawny colors with green eyes and white paws.

"As with any pair of sturdy Norse lads," Mr. Sorenson said, "they are not impervious to the lure of food. Let's put the kettle on, and then I will see to my barn chores and fetch the straggler."

The cats led the procession into the warmth of a dimly lit kitchen, clearly following a nightly routine. "Shall I light some candles?" Joy asked.

"I generally make do with one or two," Mr. Sorenson said. "Vicars are supposed to be thrifty. My housekeeper pretends it isn't so, but I frequently forage in here late at night. She mutters about very large mice, while I content myself with the occasional sandwich. I know where to find what I need, but I do try to conserve the candles."

He swung the kettle over the coals on the hearth, then poured milk from a ceramic jug into a dish and set it on the floor. The cats made growly noises as they commenced lapping at the milk.

"Now to show you the penance exacted upon me each Yuletide." He opened a cupboard above the counter and took down a large tray covered with linen.

"My housekeeper fears I will starve in her absence. We have our choice of three varieties of shortbread, cinnamon buns, lemon cake, and... I don't know what she calls this creation, but it's some sort of bread with honey, spices, nuts, and currants rolled up inside. Add a little butter or cheese, and it could fortify a marching army."

The offerings were exquisite, and the scent of cinnamon blended with other subtler spices. "She spoils you."

"I am only one man. How in a mere span of days am I to consume all of this? There's more in the larder. Fortunately, the children demand their tithes, or I would soon be fat as Mr. Walmer's prize sow. If you would slice us up some apples and cheese and choose a selection of sweets, I will see to my livestock."

Hiram would have been impersonating a plague of locusts, ill or not. "You aren't tempted to steal even a taste?"

An odd little silence tripped past, with the vicar regarding not the tray, but Joy. Or Joy's mouth. In the shadowed kitchen, she could not be sure.

"The treats will be sweeter for a little anticipation," Mr. Sorenson said. "I won't be gone long, and that,"—he nodded at a particularly ornate drawer pull—"is the tea drawer. Don't skimp on the leaves. We'll need strong tea to stand up to the baked goods."

He moved off toward the back hallway, and Joy followed him. "You haven't even a cloak."

"The animals keep the barn fairly warm, and if it's snowing, it's not all that cold."

Was he in a hurry to leave the kitchen? "That's a fallacy, and you will wear a coat, sir."

Joy grabbed a large wool cape from a peg on the wall. "This one will do." She held it open and gave it a shake.

"You scold me," he muttered, turning his back to her. "And argue with me and beat me at chess."

"You are wrong about snow and cold." Joy draped the cloak over his shoulders, yielding to the impulse to smooth fabric over muscle and bone. "I read up on northern winters before I left London. It's never too cold to snow, though it can be too dry. You tend to your own livestock?"

"I enjoy the exertion."

She was reaching to do up his buttons when he jammed a battered, low-crowned hat on his head and made for the door.

"Back in a trice."

And then he was gone into the chilly darkness. Joy put together a tea tray for two—she wasn't about to waken Hiram simply to inquire if he was hungry—in the company of two cats tending conscientiously to their ablutions.

"He spoils you," she said. "Who spoils him?" She would like to, if only a little. Pietr Sorenson was charming her without trying to. He gave as good as he got at chess. He did not stand on a pointless observation of the proprieties when people were hungry, ill, or cold. More impressive yet, he took the time to notice the fears and hurts behind the human failings in his parishioners.

"I truly would like to spoil him a little, to see him yield some of that unfailing graciousness of heart." Though how did one spoil a man who easily resisted an entire tray of sweets?

And beneath that query lay a more difficult admission: Joy liked touching Pietr Sorenson. Liked how he'd stood close to her while showing off his apothecary. Liked stealing a little caress to his shoulders while helping him to don his cloak.

She'd never been tempted to steal a caress to any part of Lord Apollo Bellingham, despite the several occasions of tactile larceny his lordship had directed toward her.

The tea kettle whistled, the cats scowled, and Joy busied herself putting together sustenance for the body. A thought intruded as she sliced two apples into quarters: What about sustenance for the heart? The vicar clearly did not want for a comfortable home or a full larder, but how did he nourish his heart?

THE LORD OF MISRULE had taken up residence in Pietr's imagination—and in his breeches.

"The problem," he muttered, picking up a muck fork and stepping into the gelding's stall, "is that contemplating the end of your role as Vicar in the Dale has unmoored you."

When private, Pietr frequently lectured himself in the second person, as if the voice in his head belonged to an internal spiritual

monitor, a stern fellow who made clear distinctions between right
and wrong.

"To be a bit at sea is understandable—change can be daunting—
but to be an utter gudgeon will not serve. Fortunately, you have yet to
toss caution entirely to the wind. And need I remind you, you house
an invalid in the person of her sot-in-training brother, and thus Miss
Danforth's wellbeing rests entirely in your hands."

The dean presiding over the cathedral of Pietr's honor droned on,
though Miss Danforth, having served several Seasons' penance in
Mayfair, was unlikely to be ignorant of worldly pleasures.

"Not that experience on her part signifies."

Pietr's lack of recent experience signified. Those infrequent trips
to take tea with the bishop had allowed for a few discreet frolics with
the widow who ran the lodging house Pietr preferred in York. On his
last visit, he'd accepted the use of the Wentworths' York town house,
and that had honestly been something of a relief.

Or had it? A relief to his conscience, perhaps, but what of his
body? What of the heart that longed for the comfort of a skin-to-skin
embrace and the soft laughter of a satisfied lover?

"And I'm hardly ancient," he observed as he finished tidying up
the horse's stall. "Hardly doddering."

Watching Joy Danforth contemplate strategy at the chessboard
had inspired Pietr to musings of a different sort. Would a kiss beneath
the mistletoe be too trite? Could he take her skating on the river, his
arm about her waist?

"Not with a foot of new snow on the ice." Though the children
would broom and shovel the ice clear within an hour of sunup. "Not
with Lord Apollo Bellingham awaiting the arrival of his guests."

Pietr paused to scratch his horse's ears. Thomas, named for the
Apostle given to doubt, was a good sort of horse, up to Pietr's weight,
equally reliable in the traces or under saddle. He was exactly the
variety of unprepossessing, stalwart fellow a servant of the Church
should own.

"But you are a gelding, my friend."

Seeing Joy Danforth padding around in Pietr's slippers, watching candlelight dance along the highlights in her unbound hair, had inspired Pietr's imagination to bolt from the barn at a dead gallop, and the beast was not headed for the churchyard.

"I want to bed her. I want *her* to bed *me*." He'd felt the occasional stir of interest in other women. Althea Wentworth had inspired mild speculation, though she'd needed a friend far more than she'd needed a complication.

"And that's all I would be to Miss Danforth. A complication." He left the stall, taking care to latch the door. Tomorrow might well see the horse and cow confined to quarters if the snow kept up, and a bored beast of any species got up to mischief.

Milking the cow took less than ten minutes. She wasn't dry yet, but her output was waning. "I will offer you warmer water tomorrow, I promise, and you might be inspired to drink more and thus yield more."

She liked a good scratch to her brow, and the chickens preferred her company to that of the horse. Pietr poured the milk into its glass jar, tended to Bossy's housekeeping, and fed supper all around. Nobody's water bucket had ice in it yet, though tomorrow morning might tell a different tale.

"Kitten, you'd best show yourself," he called when he'd finished collecting the day's eggs.

Now that the moment to return to the kitchen was at hand, Pietr hesitated. He'd made no overtures, crossed no lines, but he'd also failed utterly to lecture himself into a state of resolute decorum. Standing in the cold with his breeches undone might obliterate the most direct evidence of wayward thoughts, but it would not calm a wayward heart.

"I yearn," he said, having a look around the hay mow. No kitten. "I am out of the habit of yearning, and thus my self-discipline is wanting."

Was that a good thing? To lose sight of longings and desires that the Creator had designed into the creature?

"Kitten, I will leave you to sleep with the hens, and that is an indignity your compatriots will never allow you to live down. If you aspire to be a cathedral cat, you must locate some damned dignity."

A rustling in the straw pile presaged the emergence of the third feline to grace Pietr's barn. "Ruddy blighter. You had me worried." Such a small fellow would not fair well against the elements. Pietr scooped him up and held him at eye level.

"You would do well to contemplate your future, my boy. I have ambitions for you."

The kitten commenced purring, an inordinately comforting rumble. No ambitions here, just a healthy little creature who suffered a bit of shyness.

"I would hate to lose you," Pietr said, knowing that he must return to the kitchen, and to good sense. "But I believe Miss Danforth has put her finger on a worse problem. I have lost sight of myself."

Winter evenings had ever been a penance, when Pietr was most likely to be plagued by old memories and sorrows. He missed his wife, though that ache had grown dull with age and was softened— finally—by many joyous memories.

The problem was not missing a departed spouse, but rather, missing *himself*. The part of him that wasn't a vicar, wasn't a brother, wasn't a neighbor. The man, *the person*. The living, breathing, hungering, raging, pondering, lusting male nobody ever saw.

"The part of me that is not now and never will be a reliable, unprepossessing gelding." Where had that fellow been, and why was he choosing now to make a reappearance?

Pietr closed up the barn and braved the cold, dark walk back to the kitchen and to all the temptations and insights to be had therein.

CHAPTER FOUR

Joy was famished now that a laden tray sat on the sturdy wooden table across from the kitchen hearth. A stout black tea was steeping, and the house had acquired the profound quiet of a winter night, though the hour was early. She had braided her hair, the fire's soothing warmth at her back, and all the while, her mind had been far from quiet.

Of all men, Vicar Pietr Sorenson tempted her to foolishness.

Because he was vigorous of body and mind?

Because he was good-hearted?

Because he was forbidden?

Other men had earned her notice, though only in passing. One had a clever turn of phrase, another was an inspired dancer, a third made an excellent partner at whist. Ever since she'd ventured past propriety with a long-ago singing teacher, she'd felt little curiosity regarding how any particular man comported himself behind a closed bedroom door.

The poets lied outrageously. There were no rainbows and raptures. There was a lot of fumbling and muttering and awkwardness. Then, when the fellow had found satisfaction, worse awkwardness ensued.

The vicar had her wondering, though, about what might happen *with him* behind a closed kitchen door—fumbling and awkwardness would have no part in the proceedings, of that she was certain.

And yet, further speculations about private encounters with Pietr Sorenson were pointless. He was a gentleman, and Joy was soon to be promised to another. She nonetheless allowed herself to assist Mr. Sorenson to remove his cloak when he returned from his chores.

"I'll set that milk in the window box," she said, accepting the jug from him. "The cream will have risen in time for our morning tea."

"And we shall have plenty of eggs," he replied, taking three brown eggs from his pockets. "We had a stretch of sunny days last week, and I usually keep a lantern lit in the barn, hence the largesse. If ever you need a topic for the churchyard, bring up how well the hens are laying, and all the local philosophers will have something profound to offer on the topic."

And Pietr Sorenson would not merely pretend to listen to that wisdom, he'd give it his whole attention.

"I peeked in on Hiram," Joy said. "He's utterly cast away, though he did not seem overly warm to me." He had looked once again like a youth, a boy lost in slumber, not a man who'd completed his studies and was ready to find his place in the world.

The vicar hung up his cloak, thwacked his hat against a muscular thigh, and hung the hat on the same peg. "Perhaps a cold has him in its grip. Colds can impersonate an ague. When he's not escorting you across the tundra, what occupies young Mr. Danforth?"

"The usual amusements. He came down from university last spring and was in great demand by the hostesses. Papa and Mama have high hopes for him."

The vicar wiped his boots on the worn carpet at the back door and plowed his fingers through his hair. "Does Hiram have any aspirations for himself?"

Joy led the way back to the kitchen's warmth. The cats sat on the raised hearth, looking vaguely annoyed, as cats often did.

"Hiram aspires to affix himself upon Lord Apollo Bellingham's coattails, there to bide until an heiress or other serendipitous opportunity takes notice of him. My brother wasn't much of a scholar. He has no vocation for the Church. The military is fresh out of wars to wage, and a diplomatic post is best undertaken by those with some gift for tact."

"Your brother is a gentleman, then. They also serve, who keep the tailors employed." Mr. Sorenson washed his hands at the wet sink, then took down a hanging ham. "Would you like some meat with our repast? This is a very good smoked ham."

"I would, thank you."

First, he chopped up a generous serving for the cats, which provoked a soft mewling noise from the vicinity of his breast pocket.

"Somebody else is hungry," he said, returning the ham to its hook and the knife to a washbasin. "A great strapping lad was lurking beneath the straw pile."

He reached into his waistcoat and produced a ball of gray fur. "Behold, I bring you tidings of great joy. The resident lion deigned to come in for supper."

The lion was clearly of the same lineage as the Norse cats, right down to the luxurious coat and tufted ears. Said lion was a juvenile exponent of that grand race and wore an expression of perpetual dismay, as if the world sorely affronted one of his tender sensibilities.

"Does he have a name?"

"Köttr. Cat, in the ancient language of my mother's antecedents."

"Cat? That's the best you could do?"

"He answers to it, when there's ham involved." Mr. Sorenson set the kitten down with the larger beasts, who made room for him around the feast. "The kitten will go with me to the cathedral. The older fellows are too set in their ways, but Köttr has a vocation."

"How can you tell?"

"He's never caught a mouse. That's a sure sign of spiritual sophistication in a cat, according to Mrs. Peabody."

Köttr certainly enjoyed a good appetite. "Spiritual sophistication or laziness?"

The vicar washed his hands again, and without even being reminded to. "Is Hiram lazy?"

The cozy kitchen, the quiet, and the weight of a day that hadn't gone as planned all conspired to rob Joy of sororal loyalty.

"If Hiram is an example of what happens to decent boys sent off to university, we ought to close the doors of both Oxford and Cambridge. He did well enough at public school. He had friends whose company I could enjoy, though they were boys, with all the noise, bluster, and vulgarity attendant thereto."

Mr. Sorenson took Joy by the hand and led her to the table. "What happened at university?"

He held her chair, and she sat, then waited for him to take the place at her elbow. She'd rummaged for cutlery and table napkins and found the kitchen to be orderly and well supplied.

"Will you say the grace, Mr. Sorenson?"

"Might you call me Pietr? We are about to break bread and embark on a mutual lament regarding that blessing known as family. Tell me about Hiram, and then I will burden you regarding darling Clara."

"Grace first, please. You are the professional, after all."

His expression was fleetingly mulish, then his smile was back in place, and he took Joy's hand. "Very well. Thank you, Lord, for our dinner. But for Your bounty, we would all be much thinner."

"That was awful. Let me try." She liked holding his hand, which was surprisingly callused. She liked inane conversation about a kitten's spiritual proclivities, and she liked helping to put together simple, substantial fare.

"For shelter and compassion in the middle of a cold, dark winter, we are grateful," she said. "For sustenance of many varieties, we are grateful. For a good game of chess, with victory going to the superior force, we are exceedingly grateful. Amen." Joy kept to herself an additional prayer: If the Almighty could see fit to send at least another half foot of snow, she'd be grateful for that too.

Oh, and could Hiram please recover from whatever ailed him—in another three weeks or so?

"Tell me of your brother," the vicar—Pietr—said. "And I see you found the cider. Excellent stuff, but be warned: It has a Yorkshire kick."

"Hiram will like it, then. It's as if his course of study at Oxford was vice and venery. He learned to sneer there, to make a quip that was as cutting as it was humorous. He took up wagering and, with it, the related skill of neglecting to pay the trades."

"He'll find his way," Pietr replied. "It can take a few years of racketing about Town, a trip to the sponging house, a friendship shattered on the shoals of insult. Most of us do grow up, though. Eat something, please, or somehow, though she's off in York, my housekeeper will know we've neglected her largesse."

Joy took up a slice of the rolled-up bread with all the nuts, currants, spices, and honey inside. She'd smeared soft white cream cheese over both slices so the result was both sweet and rich.

"Hiram is only reacting to the family circumstances generally," Joy said. "I am to make an advantageous match, not so much for my own sake as to revive the family fortunes. Mama and Papa act as if Grandpapa is still steering the family ship on a course of ample and reliable revenue. Hiram knows we are in a precarious state and hasn't our parents' gift of blithe indifference."

"I'm sorry. Ruin has befallen many a respected family in recent years, but that doesn't make it any easier when it's your parents being dunned."

The situation wanted condolences, though Joy would never have admitted that.

"I spend all of my time sewing different flounces and borders on my dresses," she said. "I have redecorated the same bonnet so many times there ought not to be a pheasant feather left in England. Papa says appearances must be maintained, but I do not understand why we must maintain a theater box we seldom use. A coach and four we cannot afford. Six footmen when we can barely keep two busy. Papa says if we practice visible economies, we will no longer have credit, but I say if we had begun practicing economies five years ago, we would not need that credit."

She took a sip of her cider to ease the ache that had started in her throat, for her appetite had deserted her.

"Lord Apollo Bellingham is to save the sinking Danforth ship?"

"*I* am to save the sinking ship by marrying Lord Apollo. A time-honored solution."

Pietr ate in silence, while Joy wondered why tears threatened. Lord Apollo was not awful. He was fastidious. He was mannerly. He was well liked.

"A time-honored solution, perhaps," Pietr said, "but this solution does not honor *you*. Does Lord Apollo know your favorite book?"

"According to Lord Apollo, women who read are only slightly less annoying than women who read and insist on discussing what they read. The whole parlor found that observation worth a laugh." And Joy had smiled along with them.

"While I," Pietr said quietly, "find such humor the pathetic bleating of a small man, and don't rip up at me because I have been honest. To ignore cruelty only encourages its repetition."

His tone had taken on an uncharacteristic severity, a hint of anger. *Let not the sun go down upon your wrath.*

"It's all my fault," Joy said. "If I had exerted myself to be more charming after my come out, if I had taken, if I had secured a match... To hear Mama tell it, my wardrobe alone beggared us, and trotting me out for the annual parade has only added to our penury. I owe it to my family to make amends."

Pietr picked up her slice of bread and held it out to her. "You demanded an endless supply of new dresses? Insisted your parents host one entertainment after another? Would have only jeweled slippers for your dainty feet?"

Joy ate, for the food was good, and the conversation good too. Blunt, but good. "I wanted to take over Grandpapa's business. Papa would not hear of it, and so the enterprise was sold. Our income went with it, and what Papa thought we could manage on, with only a few tenant properties bringing in rent, I do not know."

"Did you insist on that coach and four? Insist on sending your brother to university when he could have finished a clerkship by now?"

"You might have noticed I am not very good at insisting on anything." She ate her bread and thought about that. What was the price of insisting? Mama got the vapors, Papa retreated into fuming silence, and Hiram went out drinking with his friends.

But then, on any given day, Mama had the vapors, Papa fumed, and Hiram caroused. *What am I doing, planning to marry a man who insults well-read women?*

"Tell me about the cathedral post," Joy said, "and about your sister, Clara."

Pietr put a square of shortbread on Joy's plate. "First, I will tell you that your family's circumstances are not your fault. Perhaps bad luck played a larger role than bad judgment, but from no perspective is the situation your fault. That you accept the burden thrust upon you speaks to your nobility of character."

Joy finished her cider, which was really quite good, the best she'd ever had. "Is there a but?"

"But I wish your happiness was of more moment to your family, for it certainly matters to me."

"You hardly know me." And yet, his words, so clipped and fierce, warmed her as the fire in the great stone hearth could not.

"Do you know how long it has been since I had a real chess match? Not a little exercise in moving pieces about so grown men can avoid admitting to loneliness, but a contest of wits? Do you grasp how absolutely lovely it was to walk in that back door and know I had company waiting for me in the kitchen? Intelligent, charming, and—lest we overlook the obvious—pretty company? You exude calm practicality, you are patient with and protective of your spoiled whelp of a brother, and I wish you had not braided your hair."

Joy touched her braids, affixed to her head in a simple coronet. "My hair?"

Pietr finished his slice of holiday bread, or whatever it was. "Suffice it to say, you are not a pawn to be sacrificed for the sake of the Danforth army. We should take some of this fare up to Hiram."

Pietr Sorenson was *lonely*. Despite his own calm practicality, kind heart, and genuine vocation, he was lonely. The realization comforted Joy in some odd way.

"We will see to Hiram when we are finished," Joy said. "Lord knows, he's willing to bellow for attention when he wants it. Tell me of your family and their ambitions for you."

Pietr chewed his shortbread into oblivion. Like the cats, he had the gift of conveying that he was annoyed without saying a word.

"Clara is concerned for my happiness."

"Of course she is. Tell me the rest of it."

He sighed as he peered into his empty tankard. He regarded the felines now curled side by side on the hearth with the kitten heaped atop them.

"Clara is very good at insisting."

"I don't know as I'd like her."

His smile was bleak. "I'm not sure I like her either, but with family, liking sometimes doesn't come into it. Let's split another slice of bread, shall we? Then if you would be so good as to tidy up, I'll shovel the path to the barn one last time for the night."

Anybody who knew him would probably say that Pietr Sorenson was an honest man. The honest man had just changed the subject with all the grace of a beer wagon turning on a crowded street. Joy allowed him that courtesy, because he was right: With family, liking didn't much matter, but duty did.

Alas, duty to family mattered a very great deal.

∾

CLARA WAS GOOD AT INSISTING, so good that Pietr wondered if she didn't frequently insist herself into awkward corners. She'd insisted that she and the baron would suit, for example, though the union of two strong-willed, proud people had proven a daunting challenge to them both.

She had insisted that if Pietr took a post in Greater Dungheap, Yorkshire, she would never visit him there. The village—usually referred to as Rothton, when referred to by name at all—was as pretty a hamlet as any to be found in England, and yet, Clara had never come any closer to Pietr's abode than York itself, and then only twice.

"My sibling has a knack for passionate, unrelenting argument," Pietr said as Joy sliced them off another thick serving of holiday bread. "She puts bulldogs to shame, but that doesn't mean she's wrong. I did not spend years studying biblical symbolism just to fritter away my seasons judging pie contests. She is right about that much, at least."

Joy set the knife in the sink. "Even a blind dove finds the occasional pea?"

"Clara is no dove. She has been sermonizing at me since I went up to university. I am to make the world a better place, bring glory to the Sorenson name—humble glory, of course—and do well for myself at the same time. Once I'd chosen the Church, she made her variety of peace with my decision, but my prospects have not improved to her liking."

Joy wrapped the loaf in linen and tucked it into the bread box, then slathered the slice with cream cheese. Watching her putter in Pietr's kitchen provoked an ache in his chest to go with the ache behind his falls.

All this aching was pointless, of course, but still... Was it so very wrong to have enjoyed years of peaceful service here on the edge of the moor? To have cherished the memory of a good, dear woman taken too soon?

"What of your sister's ambitions?" Joy asked, bringing the bread to the table and passing Pietr the larger half of the slice. "How has she spent her time when she's not haranguing you? More cider?"

"Two fingers will do." One went carefully with the local cider. Never on an empty stomach, never more than a couple of servings, or the next morning became an ordeal.

Joy poured the cider into his tankard, took a sip, then set the drink beside his plate and resumed her seat at his elbow. The moment was insignificant, but also domestic, intimate. Another reason to ache.

"Clara has three children in her nursery. Two boys and a girl, and they are perfectly well behaved. I fear she'd rather have a wayward horde to bring to order, but the children are sweet and clever and little trouble. I visit them every other year, and they grow taller without becoming more rebellious."

"And her husband?"

"He is already quite tall enough."

Joy made a face. "Is he perfectly well behaved?"

"They seem to have reached an accommodation. His lordship tends to his acres and commercial interests, and Clara is the gracious hostess and social partner such a man needs. He does not suffer her to intrude into his business affairs, and she rules supreme at home."

Joy took a bite of her bread. "Many couples operate in separate spheres." She spoke as if reciting a little homily, a reminder to herself not to expect too much from a husband.

"What is the point of marrying if one's spouse is to be an intimate in only the biological sense? I lack the fortitude to consign myself to such a union, but then, I am not my sister."

Joy took another sip of his cider. "To what extent is your sister hectoring you because her husband won't put up with her meddling and her children offer her little challenge? To what extent is she managing you because you are one of few pieces still in play on her board? Her children are not old enough to leave the nursery. Her husband has lowered the marital portcullis. I gather your parents are no longer extant, and your cousins reside in another country. She is a queen with very few pawns."

Clara would like being referred to as a queen, while Pietr did not like being referred to as a pawn.

"That I want to argue with you suggests you have put your finger on a difficult truth. Clara is my only sibling and my only immediate family. I alienate her at my peril, and yet, you are also correct: She is a managing woman by nature, and I am available to be managed."

Why had he allowed that? When had he made the decision to capitulate to Clara's incessant dunning? If he became the Archbishop of York, would she lament that he was not yet Archbishop of Canterbury?

"You aren't eating your bread," Joy said. "I was hungrier than I realized, and this is delicious fare."

Simple fare, but good. "My housekeeper likes to bake, and I like to eat. It's a good system, but if I'm not to acquire the dimensions of a plow horse, I'd best do some shoveling." Then too, another dose of cold air was in order. Watching Joy eat with her fingers and purloin sips of cider was playing havoc with Pietr's imagination.

"I will tidy up and make a tray for Hiram. He cannot sleep forever." She rose and gathered the plates, as if a woman intending to marry into a titled family regularly did duty as a scullery maid.

"Thank you," Pietr said. "For the company, for the conversation, for everything." For making him *think*, for making him see Clara's situation in a different light. A more complicated light and probably more accurate too.

"Nobody will steal the snow, Pietr. You need not shovel the whole path tonight. I'll wait for you to come in before I go up to the study."

"It's a short path, and I've kept after it." Some symbolism lay in that pronouncement, but Pietr was too muddled and aching to parse it out.

He hung a lantern on the lamppost at the back door, the light revealing that the footsteps he'd made earlier were already drifted over with new snow. He shoveled off the back terrace, shoveled the path to the barn, and for good measure shoveled the path to the spring house as well, though the kitchen had a pump, and nobody actually made much use of the spring house.

All that shoveling moved a lot of snow, but did nothing to ease a profound and pointless desire for Joy Danforth. She was to make a sacrificial marriage, though she probably did not use that term even in the privacy of her thoughts.

A marriage to a man who ridiculed literate women.

"Let not the sun go down upon your wrath," Pietr muttered, propping the shovel by the back door. He unhooked the lantern, stomped the snow from his boots, and made a decision.

"You are serious about your shoveling," Joy said, draping a towel over a wooden tray that held a teapot, sweets, an apple, and some cheese. "I watched you. You know what you're about."

"Shoveling snow can be meditative. Shall I carry that tray upstairs?"

"Thank you." She unfolded the blanket she'd been wearing in the study and draped it around her shoulders. "I don't want to leave this cozy kitchen."

"But you are a dutiful sister, and so up to the study you will go. I will look in on the patient with you and check on the fires in the bedrooms."

Pietr did not want to leave the kitchen either, but if he remained here with her, he'd tease from her more details of her situation with Lord Apollo. Vicars learned to extract confessions from the unsuspecting, if not the unwilling.

And then Pietr would torture himself with the information Joy revealed. He did not know Lord Apollo, but he knew of him. Lord Apollo's papa was a marquess, an exalted personage indeed, and Apollo was the spare, two years behind an unmarried brother. Joy Danforth might well become a marchioness one day, and a rural vicar had no business wishing her anything but great happiness as she turned her feet onto that path.

She banked coals that had already been thoroughly covered in ashes and pushed to the back of the hearth, then preceded Pietr up the steps. The sconces were lit, though Pietr knew his way through the house in pitch darkness.

When they reached the chilly foyer, he set the tray on the sideboard. "May I ask you to tarry with me for a moment, Joy?"

"You may." She rubbed the condensation from the window and peered out across the green. "The inn looks so cozy, but I can't see the path anymore."

"Joy?"

She turned a puzzled expression on him. "Pietr?"

"I would like to give you something, but only if you can accept it as a gift rather than endure it as a presumption."

"This sounds serious."

And Pietr had not meant to be serious. "I would like to kiss you. I would like to offer a gesture of esteem, of masculine regard, but not if you will be offended."

Her brows knit, and he wanted to trace them with his nose.

"I will not be offended."

"You must not also be forbearing, Joy. Don't *tolerate* a kiss from me. I want you to enjoy it, to enjoy *yourself*. I want you to have one moment for pleasure. You deserve at least that, and—"

She put her fingers to his lips. "I understand."

He wrapped her hand in his. "You do?"

"I am not yet promised to anybody. You are not yet indentured to the cathedral. Today has been splendid, when it might have been very un-splendid. I like you, Pietr Sorenson, and I esteem you as well."

She opened the blanket and enfolded him in its warmth. He resisted the urge to rush, to grab and dash, and instead slipped his arms around her and gathered her close. She came into his embrace by degrees, first wrapping her arms around him, then leaning on him a little, then settling against him.

The pleasure of holding her, of physical closeness, was as intoxicating as hard cider, wassail, and winter ale combined, and so much richer. Joy Danforth lacked height, she did not lack curves.

Pietr felt Brobdingnagian compared to her, and so very, delightfully male.

His body rejoiced, and that he still had the knack—of delighting in the female shape, of treasuring female trust—delighted his soul too.

"I will think of you on snowy nights for the rest of my life, Pietr Sorenson." Joy paused with her lips a half inch from his. "They will be precious, happy thoughts."

He had the discipline to pause with her, to register the luscious scent of the cloved oranges, the soft warmth of the wool blanket enveloping them, the profound quiet of a darkened house on a winter night. Then he closed his eyes and gave himself up to the pleasure of cherishing a woman for the first time in far, far too long.

And as Joy kissed him back, he was engulfed in the pleasure of being cherished in return.

JOY HAD DEVELOPED AN UNTESTED THEORY. Tucked close to Pietr Sorenson, his lips moving gently on hers, her theory was confirmed.

Lord Apollo Bellingham, man among men, the envy of his age, favorite of the angels, and pattern card of masculine perfection, could not kiss worth a damn.

Mr. Hanley-Bledsoe, that long-ago singing teacher who had been a wonder at the keyboard and with *bel canto* repertoire, had been similarly lacking in talent when it came to kissing—and likely when it came to much else that Joy had allowed him.

Or quite possibly, Pietr Sorenson had virtuoso skill as a lover. He did not grope, he caressed. He did not mash his mouth against hers, he invited and tempted. He did not make odd noises reminiscent of tired bullocks flopping into the straw, he inspired Joy to soft sighs of longing.

She would have been content to stand in the shadowy foyer delighting in Pietr's kisses all night, except that Hiram waited in the study, and beyond that... She might as well have been faced with crossing the drifted moor on foot at night. That thought inspired her to take a taste of her partner-in-pleasure, to trace the shape of his bottom lip with her tongue.

A chess match ensued, full of sallies and feints, teasing and more temptation, until unmistakable evidence of masculine desire rose against Joy's middle. She had done that, filled a man with yearning *for her*. Mr. Hanley-Bledsoe—she'd forgotten his first name if she'd ever known it—had come at her with his bayonet already fixed, so to speak. In recent years, she'd wondered how many other pupils he'd impaled and if seducing young ladies was a form of revenge for never having been successful on the stage.

She was done wondering about Mr. Handy Blade. For the rest of her life, she'd be wondering about Pietr Sorenson. Where had he learned to rub a lady's earlobe like that? When had he become so adept at cradling the back of her head against his palm, such that she wanted to arch into his touch like a demanding cat?

"We must stop," Pietr whispered. "*I* must stop."

He did not stop, fortunately, for Joy felt an equal compulsion to prolong the kiss. To trace the contours of his muscular back, to learn the precise texture of his hair. While the kitchen and study were adequately heated, only in Pietr's arms was she finally warm.

"Joy, we cannot... We must not."

"We'll cease, then," Joy said, relaxing against him, "but do not apologize. I had wondered."

He stroked her hair, his lips grazing her temple. "About?"

"Was there something wrong with me that the pleasures a proper woman eschews outside of marriage have failed to move me?"

He peered down at her. "You are moved?"

"You have moved me, heaven, and earth, Pietr. Your sister is right that you are wasted here in rural obscurity. You should have a post as the royal kisser of wayward spinsters."

He kissed her again, and what did it say that two kisses into the conversation, Joy already knew what he was trying to communicate.

Pleasure at her words, and regret too. He and she might share more than two kisses, but only a few more, and only kisses.

"I'm sorry," he said. "Kisses should move, and that you've had to put up with the other kind is a poor reflection on those who've kissed you."

She rested her forehead against his chest. "I put up with much more than kisses, Pietr. If there is such a thing as a wayward spinster, I am she." This was the oddest, most wonderful conversation. Like the cider and the holiday bread. Unexpectedly delightful, given the circumstances.

"There is no such thing as a wayward spinster. There are only people with a healthy sense of curiosity about pleasures the Almighty designed into us. I'm sorry you were a disappointed spinster, if you qualify as any sort of spinster at all."

"You aren't dismayed?"

"I stand in your embrace, ready to procreate, Joy Danforth. If I am dismayed, it's not because you indulged in a few discreet adventures. You would be amazed at how many first babies in my parish show up less than nine months after the nuptials. Half, at least, and my congregation knows not to remark upon that in my hearing. If the Christmas story teaches us nothing else, we should know that any mother and child safely through their travail is cause for profound rejoicing."

Well, that explained it. Pietr Sorenson tarried in the wilderness because his wrath was provoked by hypocrisy. People who put on airs and demanded perfection of their daughters while indulging in all manner of debauchery and nearly expecting licentiousness of their sons would drive him barmy.

People who never missed services lest they lose a chance to spread malicious gossip in the churchyard would have him hurling verbal thunderbolts from the pulpit.

People who maintained an empty theater box while expecting the cobbler and his family to go hungry would wound Pietr's heart.

The very society Joy had been raised to value above all else wore a different aspect when viewed through the eyes of a man who took his honor seriously.

"I wish," Joy said, then fell silent. Wishing was pointless.

"Tell me."

"I wish I had met you much earlier and that spring was not inevitable."

"We can share those wishes," he said, easing away. "And probably a few more best left to the imagination."

"Many more."

They shared a smile instead, a little sad, but also pleased and intimate. Pietr reached above Joy's head, and when she thought he'd pluck a berry from the mistletoe dangling from the crossbeam, he instead took down the whole bunch.

"I will see to the fires in the bedrooms," he said, "and then join you in the library."

Joy realized with a start that he needed time to compose himself. He was as discommoded as she was, probably doubting his decision to take the cathedral post.

Well, good. He belonged here, where he was happy. She would have told him that, except he'd taken the mistletoe with him into the gloom of the upper floor.

Joy stayed below, wrapped in her blanket and in wishes that would never come true.

CHAPTER FIVE

Pietr slept badly.

He'd taken his frustrated desire in hand, so to speak, before rejoining Joy and Hiram in the study. She had read to them from the offerings of the Lake poets, her voice a soothing rivulet of verse. Spring lambs, daffodils, clouds... symbols of new life and hope, though Pietr heard them as proof of that inevitability she'd mentioned.

New life was all well and good for spring lambs, but what was wrong with the old life for Rothton's vicar? Precisely nothing, and yet, Pietr was taking up his Bible and his kitten—neither one much comfort of late—and leaving the village for a lot of glorified clerking. But then, what was glorious about judging pie contests or listening to Mrs. Peabody's endless fretting?

Kissing Joy Danforth was glorious.

"You have morning callers." The lady herself had stuck her head into the study. "They would not come into the house."

The vicarage was redolent of cinnamon, for Joy was of a mind to try one of Mrs. Baker's recipes. The result was warmth throughout the vicarage such as Pietr did not usually enjoy in his housekeeper's absence. Hiram dozed away the morning in his bedroom, while Pietr had tried to work on a sermon.

The weather had eased up, though low clouds hung in a sullen overcast, and more than a foot of new snow had fallen.

"Guests?" Pietr did not want to contend with guests, or not guests come to spy.

"They said they are reporting for duty."

"Ah, not guests, then. My angels." He rose, happy to leave the wisdom of the prophets for the wisdom of the snow shovel. "The village boys and girls with more high spirits than their parents can endure. We have a system, the parents and I."

"There are a good dozen of them," Joy said. "They appear to be in very high spirits. I hope your system involves building snow forts on the green or something equally industrious."

She wore a full-length apron, and her hair was gathered up in a chignon. A streak of flour crossed one cheek, and her cuffs had been turned back. Pietr could easily imagine that the kitchen where she'd spent half the morning conjuring sweets was hers, and that he was hers too. He could not for the life of him keep this week's scriptural passage in his head.

Something about the blind receiving sight and the lame walking. Not a word for a randy vicar smitten with a woman who played chess almost as well as she kissed.

"My system involves selfless acts of charity," he said. "The greater good and children surviving until Christmas."

He went to the front door, grabbed his coat, and stepped outside. "Children, good morning."

A chorus of "good morning, Vicar" greeted him.

"We have much work to do. Thomas and Bartholomew, you will handle the church steps and walkways. Beatrice and Alexander, Mrs. Peabody's walkway awaits you. Haley and Buford, you will tend to the Wiles's household." He went on handing out assignments, until only two stalwarts remained, the smallest of the lot.

"What about us, Vicar?" Mary Ellen Lumley asked. "Sissy and I want to shovel too."

They were twins, all of six years old. One was fair, the other dark, and they had eight siblings and another on the way. The Lumley marriage was happy, or as happy as a family of ten could be with limited means.

"You have a special job," Pietr said, kneeling before them. "I have tried to keep up with my own paths and walkways, but the job isn't complete. I need the path to the barn swept, you see."

"Swept?"

"Right down to the grass. The terrace and back steps too. If I should fall upon my backside while carrying the eggs and milk, I would be a very hungry fellow. Come, I'll show you."

They trooped through the house, gawking at the art on the walls, some of which had been done by their older siblings. One of the older Lumley boys—Silas—had an exceptionally good eye. Pietr had arranged for him to learn some proper drawing technique from Her Grace of Rothhaven, who had pronounced the boy a prodigy.

"Is this what heaven smells like?" Mary Alice asked.

"I hope heaven is warm like this," Mary Ellen said. "And that no babies cry in heaven."

"Is Amos unwell?" The youngest was barely a year old and already walking.

"Teething, Mama says," Mary Ellen replied, following Pietr down the steps. "Teething is loud."

"Amos teethes a lot," Mary Alice added.

Pietr had tended to the path immediately after consuming the breakfast Joy had prepared. Toast, eggs, ham... Despite being a lady of gentle birth, she'd apparently learned her way around a kitchen of necessity. She'd said her family's cooks tended to quit without notice, and yet, her parents nonetheless expected omelets and toast to appear in the breakfast parlor every morning without fail.

Let not the sun go down upon your wrath.

Pietr equipped the girls with brooms and repeated his usual

admonishments: *Battling the elements is taxing. Take frequent breaks. Don't stay outside too long. To do the job right is more important than to finish first. Keep a watchful eye on your fellow laborer's safety, for the Lord sent forth His apostles in twos for reasons.*

"If Mary Alice falls on her arse, I will help her up," Mary Ellen said earnestly.

"Good girl, and I'm sure Mary Alice will do the same for you."

He left them discussing plans for whether to sweep from barn to house or house to barn, or to meet in the middle, though he returned bearing two scarves.

"One wants to be properly dressed for such an important job." The little girls held still while he swaddled little necks, ears, and chins in Clara's handiwork. "Better?"

"Smells like heaven," Mary Alice said.

"Like heaven and Christmas." Mary Ellen took up her broom. "We'll get to work now. We don't want the big boys to eat all the shortbread."

"I would never allow that. Come inside before you get cold. That's an order."

"Yes, Vicar." They grinned and capered off down the steps.

Pietr's yard would acquire a few snow angels in the next half hour, and the beasts in the barn would have callers. Nothing for it, but he must return to beating his head against Scripture and praying for inspiration. People expected a weekly dose of comfort and wisdom, every Sunday without fail, but the longer Pietr stared at the blank pages on his blotter, the more he longed for some comfort and wisdom himself.

Rather than return to the library, he found himself in the kitchen, the one place in the house where Mrs. Baker had not bothered to hang mistletoe. No matter, for the sight of Joy Danforth in her apron had Pietr's imagination festooned with the stuff.

"The children think you've conjured a whiff of heaven." As did Pietr, and not only with her baking.

"The cinnamon buns have just come out of the oven. I'm mixing up the icing."

"Then the oven is still hot?"

Joy swiped at her cheek with the back of her hand, and the smudge of flour disappeared. "It will be for hours. I was thinking of trying my hand at the holiday bread."

"First, I need to bake a batch of potatoes."

"Potatoes?"

"Pocket warmers for the children to take home with them. If you distribute cinnamon buns as well, you will be canonized in a dozen little hearts."

He fetched a dozen sizable potatoes from the pantry, washed them, and arranged them in the baking oven. This was part of the system—part of *his* system—for in the households these children came from, a morning's steady exertion would earn them no additional sustenance.

"You've organized a charity shoveling brigade?"

"Years ago. I teach the children to skate because they need to get outside even in cold weather lest their parents do them an injury. Besides, I like to skate, and life cannot be relentless drudgery. One of the older boys asked if he could shovel my walkways in appreciation, and at the time, we had neither curate nor sexton. My walkways should not take precedence over those of the local widows and invalids, though I was happy enough to share the work at the church. The rest evolved, and now we have a local tradition."

Joy stirred a drizzle of milk into a bowl of sugar. "Do you pay them?"

"How is one to learn thrift if one never has any coin to manage? They earn a penny apiece for a good snowfall, plus a snack."

"And a large potato."

"The walk home is cold."

"And did I, or did I not, see you wrap up those little girls in wool scarves?"

Pietr swiped a finger through the sweet glaze. "Clara sends me at least a half-dozen scarves a year. I have only the one neck. This is delicious."

"I purloined a few drops of vanilla from Mrs. Baker's stores. I hope she won't miss it."

"Lady Nathaniel Rothmere has a cook in her employ who has studied in Paris. Monsieur Henri has quite elevated our palates, and invitations to Lynley Vale are more precious than rubies. The vanilla was doubtless a gift from her ladyship."

"To those children, I suspect your potatoes are more precious than rubies." Joy gave her icing a few more brisk stirs with a wooden spoon. "They probably start praying for snow in August."

"In summer, we keep them busy sweeping walkways, tidying up the graveyard, and weeding the flower beds on the green."

She dabbed a layer of thick white glaze onto the first bun, which had been turned out of the pan to cool on a wire rack. "Your green has flower beds?"

"We do now. Our local duke is an expert at flower gardening. I suggested we turn to him for advice, and his reply was a wagonload of bulbs, bushes, and gardening equipment, along with diagrams for how to lay out the plots. He even ventured from his hall to oversee the planting."

Joy moved to the next bun. "You asked *a duke* for gardening advice?"

"His Grace was the logical source, having spent years tending personally to one of the most exquisite walled gardens you will ever see. Rothhaven gets down on his knees and digs in the dirt, and as is known to every gardener, a man regularly on his knees is closer to both heaven and earth. Rothhaven's flowers are as wondrous as Monsieur Henri's eclairs."

Joy dabbed icing on a third bun, and why this sight provoked erotic longings, Pietr did not know. Until yesterday, he'd been a man content, a man at peace with the world and with his body. Now he envisioned her dabbing icing *on him* and licking it off, slowly.

"Does your sister, Clara, know you organize charitable shoveling brigades and employ a duke as the village gardener?"

"We would never presume to employ His Grace."

"Rothhaven the Recluse," Joy said. "He's whispered of even in London. The rumors are that he's mentally unbalanced, but his family has closed ranks to protect him from meddling."

"He's epileptic," Pietr said. "This is no secret in the local surrounds. His affliction has befallen him during services, but he attends regularly nonetheless. His family closes ranks to ensure his safety. The saddle he rides in is nearly impossible to fall out of. The walkways on his estate feature a lot of benches and no protruding rocks. He and his duchess are ferociously protective of each other. I like them both and have asked His Grace to manage my investments."

Joy passed Pietr the wooden spoon. "You are planning to snitch again, so you might as well earn your treat. I do not believe another vicar in the whole of England has prevailed on the local duke to manage both the village flower gardens and his investments. But this is what you do, isn't it? You see how somebody can make a contribution, whether by carving fantastic birds or mixing up fishy-smelling hair tonics to delight your mousers. And these people don't even know they are being coaxed away from their troubles."

Pietr dabbed icing onto a bun. The result didn't look nearly as delectable as the three Joy had done. "I am the vicar. I am given the sacred charge of looking out for the community's wellbeing. Bleating off about Scripture isn't always the best way to go about that. Spouting Scripture, in fact, can have the opposite effect. I am no good at this."

"You are brilliant at being the vicar of Rothton, Pietr. You have built a cathedral here, and your sister has no idea of the temple you've constructed out of love, common sense, tenacity, and native wit. The parishioners have fallen in with your schemes—how could they not? —but without you to shovel the path and pass out the potatoes, the edifice will not be half so sturdy or grand."

She kissed him, while his spoon dripped icing onto the table, shrieks of childish laughter came from the backyard, and some fool thumped on the front door.

This is heaven. This right here, in my kitchen, with this woman, on this cold, gray day, is heaven.

"I'd best see who that is," Pietr said, surrendering his spoon and stepping back. "Bad weather can bring on all sorts of ailments and even childbirth. Save me at least one bun, please, and expect a dozen children to descend within an hour or so."

He bussed her cheek, stole another finger of icing, and departed before he gave in to the temptation to steal more than that.

Much more.

A DAY COULD BE LEAVENED with kisses as a loaf of bread was leavened with yeast. This was a revelation to Joy, who'd regarded kissing as a male fixation to be tolerated previous to tolerating other male fixations—groping, fumbling, and lowing like a bovine, for example.

How little she'd known. How little she'd settled for, when it came to her own longings. What had she been fixated upon, such that where desire should have been, she'd mustered only curiosity, or the need to rescue her family's fortunes?

Pietr Sorenson had kissed her in the kitchen and in the little barn. He'd kissed her in the chilly foyer, and the previous evening, he'd kissed her sweetly, almost chastely, outside her bedroom door. How she'd been tempted to invite him through that door...

"We can explain an extra night en route," Hiram said, waving his hand before the study's window. "But two? Three? You're already long in the tooth, Joy. Frittering away the holidays at this poky little parsonage will not advance your cause with Lord Apollo at all. More to the point, it won't advance *my* cause."

The sudden motion of Hiram's wave at the window startled the birds away from the feeder, though they came winging back in ones and twos.

"You are feeling better," Joy said, "for which I am grateful, Hiram, but one day's bedrest isn't enough to recover from an illness that had you nearly swooning in the street."

"Two days. We arrived on Tuesday. Wednesday is half gone, and you refuse to pack up and be on our way because of a little snow. This is Yorkshire, need I remind you. In December, Yorkshire takes on the aspect of the Ninth Circle of Dante's Hell. Frozen, bitter cold. You knew that when you agreed to make this journey."

"When exactly did anybody solicit my agreement to travel? I came down to supper one night and was presented with a fait accompli, Mama's acceptance of the invitation already in the post."

Hiram's expression was amused and a little peevish. "Nor did I agree to escort you, but a decree went out from Mama and Papa that we were to be taxed with this trek, so here we are. It's time to leave, Joy. I am your brother and your escort, and you will do as I say. We'll depart after the noon meal."

Not yet, she wanted to retort, *not so soon.* "I have gone one full day without ordering my thoughts and prayers to comport with the aspirations of Lady Apollo Bellingham, Hiram. I cannot recall when I've found a span of twenty-four hours more enjoyable."

"You like to play cook. What of it?"

When had Hiram become so nasty? "I like to make a contribution, the same as anybody with a scintilla of self-respect does, but what contribution does Lord Apollo make?"

Hiram turned from the window, his arms folded as if he were a governess frustrated by a dull pupil. "He will contribute to your settlements, Joy, and that is all you need to know. His consequence will keep Papa's creditors quiet, as well as my own. His connections will open doors for me, and by this time next year, I could be wed to a suitable heiress. You might aspire to wipe a dozen sticky little faces at the vicar's kitchen table, but my ambitions run in more genteel directions."

Heaven defend the suitable heiresses from a match with Hiram. "Genteel directions, such as cockfights, horse races, drunkenness, and debauchery?"

"You begrudge me a few manly amusements." He scrubbed his hands through his hair and over unshaven cheeks. "I can't spend every waking hour standing up with wallflowers or escorting you and Mama to one silly at home after another."

No, but you could have taken on a clerkship. Could have read law. Could have tried the Church. Could have picked up an extra language in hopes of gaining a diplomatic post.

"Where do you expect to meet your suitable heiress, if not at such an at home, Hiram?"

He taunted the birds again. "At the Bellingham family seat, of course. This is a holiday gathering, and surely cousins and neighbors of all the best sorts will be on hand. I will be the much coveted bachelor just up from London. Pack your things, Joy. We are leaving after lunch."

Hiram would have stalked from the room, except that Pietr Sorenson stood in the doorway, his expression stern enough to grace the visage of a biblical patriarch.

"You do not address your sister thus," he said, advancing into the room. "Joy is a lady, and you are charged with her comfort and protection."

"She is stubborn," Hiram retorted. "I know her better than you do, Sorenson, and she wants firm guidance."

"I know Yorkshire winters, Danforth, and while the first post coach has finally made it out from York, we've had no traffic from the west. There's not a wagon track to be seen in the direction you're heading, and your coachman already got you lost once. Risk your own neck for the sake of your marital ambitions, but you will not be so cavalier with your sister's safety."

Thank God. Thank God and Pietr Sorenson. Joy had honestly feared the journey, given all the fresh snow.

"Not even a post coach?" Hiram replied.

"If a foot of snow fell here, then the moors and dales might have seen twice that. The drifts reach higher than your head, and only a blethering fool would chance those odds with a habitually drunk London coachy. You are so blinded by the opportunity to socialize with a marquess's family that you lose sight of the only sibling you have." He treated Hiram to a perusal that made those drifted dales look toasty by comparison. "My prayers will include a request to the Almighty that you grow up sooner rather than later."

Hiram blinked. He cleared his throat. He sent Joy a fulminating look. "Then I suppose we wait until traffic has resumed from the west, but only until then. I will take a tray in my room for luncheon."

"Then you will fetch that tray yourself," Pietr said. "Joy has waited on you hand and foot while you slept off shameful intemperance and a passing cold. Tend to your own needs and consider thanking your sister for her many kindnesses to you."

Hiram's masculine pride apparently could not countenance such an indignity. "I have only Joy's best interests at heart, Sorenson. Matters for the Danforth family have reached a very bad pass, worse than she knows. Much depends on her success with Lord Apollo."

"How bad?" Joy asked.

"The sum of our debts is appalling, Joy. Papa tried his hand at investing. It did not go well, and Mama is accustomed to certain amenities. I shudder to think what will befall us if you can't bring Lord Apollo up to scratch."

"So you are frightened," Pietr said, a reasoning note creeping past the frost in his voice. "You are anxious for your family and for yourself. A gentleman's education has prepared you for little else besides idleness, and your worries make it harder to think clearly. Lord Apollo may not offer for your sister, despite her best efforts to win his esteem. He is a marquess's spare and likely a creature of whim and fancy. What will you do if he decides to favor some duke's granddaughter with his suit instead?"

Frightened. The word bore a bracing whiff of truth as pungent as the fresh pine greenery adorning the vicarage's eaves.

The fleeting panic in Hiram's eyes confirmed that he was both afraid for his future and appalled that anybody should see his fear.

"I am worried too," Joy said. "I grasp the seriousness of the situation, Hiram, probably more accurately than you think. But if it's not safe to travel, it's simply not safe, and nobody can blame you for exercising basic prudence on my behalf. The Bellingham family seat has been in the north for four hundred and sixty-seven years. Lord Apollo will not fault your caution."

She nearly added, *I will bring a tray to your room,* except that she'd brought Hiram enough trays. Too many trays, truth be told.

"One can only hope that's the case," he said. "I'll have a lie-down now. All this contention has given me a ferocious headache."

If a man new to his majority could flounce, Hiram flounced out of the room.

"I hope you won't go after him," Pietr said, closing the door. "He was being an ass. I was tempted to rap him on the nose with a rolled-up newspaper, except he'd take out his ill humor on you."

"You put your finger on the problem. Hiram is facing serious grown-up problems, but he hasn't the grown-up tools to deal with them. He was too young to learn the business from Grandpapa. Papa never steered him toward a profession, and his friends are all of the class that doesn't need a profession. He is stranded on the moor, but I had not seen that."

"If he's truly desperate, I could use a curate," Pietr said. "They tend not to last here, but we appreciate them while they're on hand and feed them prodigiously well. Speaking of which, I made lunch. A baked omelet based on one of Monsieur's recipes."

Joy went to him, because the door was closed and because they had so little time. She did not castigate herself for slipping her arms around his waist.

"Thank you for making lunch, but you need not change the subject for fear I'm upset. Hiram is a problem, and the solution to his problem is apparently Lord Apollo's good offices. I don't want to leave here." *Do not want to leave you.*

Already, Pietr's embrace felt like home.

"I don't want you to go. I doubt the post coach will come through from the west today, but I'd be very surprised if we don't hear the horn blast tomorrow by midday."

"We have another day, then."

He stroked her back, stealing much of the tension from her body and none of the sorrow from her heart.

"The holiday assembly is tomorrow, Joy. I was hoping you'd stay for that. We waltz once a quarter here in the provinces, and I long to waltz with you."

"I would enjoy that." An understatement, not quite a lie. Were it possible, she would treasure the memory of publicly partnering him for the rest of her days and nights. She eased away, pleased to see that the feeder was once more adorned with birds.

"Let's eat," she said. "I never realized what a busy place a vicarage is. You have had a steady stream of callers."

Pietr let Joy change the subject. He let her go when she eased away. Tomorrow, saint that he was, he'd doubtless let her climb into the coach and make her way to the Bellingham family seat, if the weather obliged.

Lunch was good and simple, making use of the peculiar abundance of eggs so late in the year. Pietr acquainted Joy with more of the stories of the folk who'd called at the parsonage that morning. Mrs. Peabody had brought by her signature recipe for hot plasters, in case the young man was still doing poorly.

Mr. Weller had dropped off an old Latin primer, because the village boys who studied with the vicar might be able to use it. The call had lasted half an hour, while Weller had put away three servings of brandy and remarked on how he wished he'd been able to join his daughter's family for the holidays.

Mr. Petrie was missing his sons, gone to America to earn their fortunes.

The Lumley twins had come by offering to sweep the back porch again. Their gracious generosity had been accepted, though the back porch was all but bare of snow. Pietr had sent them on their way a quarter hour later, pockets stuffed with potatoes and each twin clutching half a loaf of holiday bread wrapped in a table napkin.

"You are pensive," Pietr said, rising to take dishes to the sink. "Or have I bored you with my recitation of the local edition of Debrett's?"

"I am full of good food. You mention Debrett's. Is it possible I know your sister?"

"Her husband is Lord Beacham, and she does spend her Seasons in London. Summer holidays include a trip to Denmark every other year, and Beacham conscientiously votes his seat, though Clara doesn't care for London in winter."

Beacham. Lady Beacham... The name was familiar. "We've been introduced. She is formidable. Also very handsome."

"I love her dearly," Pietr said, "but formidable is accurate too. She doesn't trade on Mama's royal connections, but then, she doesn't need to. Shall we finish off the meal with a lemon biscuit?"

He loved his lemon biscuits. Mrs. Baker had left him a good supply too.

"Shortbread will do for me."

Their hands brushed as Pietr passed her the sweet, and Joy felt the fleeting contact like a blow to the heart.

I do not want to leave this place.

I do not want to leave this man.

"How will you spend your afternoon?" she asked, taking a bite of her shortbread.

"I might spend it pummeling a worthy opponent at chess, if you're interested."

I'm interested, heaven help me. "You have calls to make, don't you?"

He popped half a lemon biscuit into his mouth. "How did you know?"

"Because you are that sort of vicar. You will look in on the elders after a heavy snow, make sure they have coal, and take them some of Mrs. Baker's largesse. You will casually shovel off any snowy walkways the children missed and make sure the widows and widowers have a way to get to the assembly. For new parents, you'll make a different sort of call. Brief, mostly reconnaissance, and you will set the elders to knitting blankets and shawls for the family of the new arrival."

He smiled, once again putting Joy in mind of a Viking. "I will meddle, to use the more accurate term. I enjoy meddling, and I'm good at it. I will miss our chess match, though."

And he did not mean he'd miss a few games that very afternoon. "Might I pay your calls with you?"

He set down the uneaten half of his biscuit. "You wish to come with me?"

"I have baked as much as I can stand to. The house will be warm for the next two days. Hiram is poor company, and I'd like to enjoy what sunshine we have."

Pietr's smile turned bashful. "I would delight in having your company this afternoon, Joy. You are right. We must make the most of what sunshine we have. Bundle up, and don't expect to be home before dark."

Joy passed her afternoon dandling babies, discussing bonnets and tisanes, and admiring Pietr Sorenson, a lovely way to pass a few hours on a chilly winter day. She did not once consider what Lady Apollo Bellingham would have done with those hours.

She did not wonder, she did not care, and she was not Lady Apollo Bellingham yet.

CHAPTER SIX

The afternoon sped by too quickly, and as Pietr watched, Joy charmed everybody she met. She listened earnestly while Mr. Wiles explained the various knives needed to carve each individual bird. She clapped in happy appreciation when one of the younger Lumleys slogged the entire distance through an alphabet of approximately twenty-two letters.

She sat with old Mrs. Peeler and admired her knitting, while Pietr filled up the coal buckets and chopped kindling. He got more shoveling, sweeping, chopping, and water hauling done in one afternoon than he could have in three days of polite calls on his own. Joy had known, ten minutes into each visit, to shoo him away to "make himself useful" while she enjoyed some friendly conversation.

Mrs. Baker's largesse, and Joy's as well, had been distributed, and Pietr had never enjoyed tending to his flock more.

"At least if the sun must set early, it does so spectacularly," Joy said. "How many of those birds did you purchase from Mr. Wiles?"

"A few." A half dozen. "They are exquisite, and one village can only use so many drawer pulls, doorknobs, newel posts, and so forth. The oldest Lumley boy paints the birds, and the younger Wiles children are all learning to carve as their father does. They have the capacity for much more production. I simply need to find them customers."

Joy walked through the churchyard beside him, the paths all tidy and clean. To the west, the sky had turned crimson, orange, and mauve, while the temperature went from frigid to shockingly cold.

How Pietr longed to take her hand, and not because the way could become slippery.

She grasped his arm about the elbow, as if she'd divined his thoughts. "To suspend the carved birds on silk threads, as if flying about, was your idea?"

"I was idling at my desk one day, watching the birds at the feeder, grateful for how much delight they give me. What of the people in the towns and cities? They do battle with rumbustious pigeons, or see swans in the parks, but the finches, nuthatches, and robins don't frequent those surrounds in great numbers. It occurred to me that the Wiles family could alleviate that sad poverty. I suggested the idea, and Mr. Wiles gave it form. The prototype—three doves and some olive branches—hangs in our church vestry."

"You will send out his work as Christmas gifts?"

"To my sister, to my bishop—a parting gift—and to my former in-laws. Our ducal families have put in orders as well, and I hope the Wileses will have a somewhat merrier Christmas this year than in years past."

Despite the cold, Pietr was in no hurry to reach the vicarage, and apparently neither was Joy.

"What of your Christmas, Pietr? You have a genius for seeing how all things can work together for the good, but what of your good? Will you spend Christmas alone?"

She'd quoted Romans, a difficult passage. "I will be besieged with visitors, and I will of course attend the Boxing Day open houses hosted by our ducal families. They are lavishly generous, and we are fortunate that both dukes are in residence at present. There are rumors that even Rothhaven will put in an appearance at tomorrow's assembly."

"Like Father Christmas?"

"Like our beloved duke in residence. He prefers Yorkshire to London, unlike His Grace of Walden. Walden is clearly daft. Ask any soul in Blackwell's common room. They will tell you the same."

"You love those souls in the common room," Joy said, "and more to the point, they love you. Why are you leaving this place, Pietr?"

They had reached the vicarage, but Pietr was reluctant to go inside. Hiram was in there, doubtless fretting and muttering, peering through the curtains at the traffic passing through the innyard. Going inside would mean the day's activities were coming to a close. All that remained was an evening meal, some reading, and then this wonderful, sweet, miraculous day would be at an end.

"I am coming to see that I took the post at the cathedral because I have been lonely here."

Joy paused on the front porch as the sunset faded from fiery hues to peaches and grays. "And you think at the cathedral, where only Köttr will know you, that you will be less lonely?"

"I wasn't thinking." Ideas connected in Pietr's mind as words formed to express them. "I have found no family of my own here. No wife, no children. I can pass out acres' worth of baked potatoes and christen every little soul born to this village, but in some way, as long as I rattle around that vicarage in solitude, I am a man apart. I belong to all of them and to none of them. I am weary of being a man apart."

Was it self-pity to admit the truth? To finally admit the truth?

"In my family," Joy said, leaning against his side, "I am the woman apart. My family doesn't think. They don't see the consequences of their actions. I have begun to join Papa for his meetings with the solicitors because I don't trust them. I manage what staff we have. I inspect the work they do lest they take advantage of Mama's poor nerves. Lady Apollo Bellingham will never have to count the silver. She will never have to ration the coal. She will never have to ask a scullery maid how to make bread. I complain of privileges, I know, but I, too, am weary."

"I will soon have been here for twenty years," Pietr said, wrapping an arm around Joy's waist. "I asked myself, Will I spend another twenty years here, feeding birds and wishing? Fashioning polite replies to Clara's carping letters? I committed myself to the post at the cathedral in what I hoped was an act of faith rather than despair, and now events have taken on the momentum of change."

"Precisely," Joy said. "Events have taken on the momentum of change for me as well. My family has pinned all of their hopes upon my becoming Lady Apollo Bellingham, a consummation devoutly to be wished, but, Pietr, I don't think her ladyship will be very happy. She will make herself content and useful. Her station will be the envy of many, but I can promise you she will have regrets too. Profound regrets."

The encroaching darkness and the overhang of the porch roof ensured they had privacy, even from curious eyes spying across the green. When Joy went up on her toes to kiss Pietr, he allowed himself to kiss her back. When she stepped away precious moments later, he let her go.

"I'll find us something for supper," Joy said. "I know how to fry bread in egg batter. With butter and honey, it's adequate fare. Hiram will want ham with his."

I'm not hungry—for food. "That sounds delightful. I'll be down to the kitchen to help in a moment."

"To help and to snitch." She bussed his cheek and slipped through the door.

Pietr needed the cold air—kissing Joy was the surest aphrodisiac he had ever encountered—and he wanted to keep an eye on the weather. Alas for him, stars were already winking into view on the eastern horizon. The night would be clear, bitter, and magnificent, but not a single snowflake was likely to fall from the sky anytime soon.

HIRAM HAD TRIED at supper to make conversation, but his topics of choice had been Lord Apollo's matched grays, Lord Apollo's hunting box in Oxfordshire, and Lord Apollo's fine town house in London.

Pietr had appeared patiently amused, while Joy had nearly pitched her plate at her brother's head. She'd peeked into Debrett's after supper and looked up Lord and Lady Beacham. Hiram had, of course, assumed she was brushing up in anticipation of the august company to be encountered at the Bellingham family seat.

Joy had passed him the book and retired for the night rather than cosh him with the peerage he so slavishly admired. Her bedroom was warm thanks to Pietr's consideration, and her wash water was warm as well. Her heart, however...

The parsonage was large enough to accommodate a sizable family, though several of the bedrooms were empty. The guest rooms were by contrast comfortably appointed, and Joy could thus assess her reflection in the folding mirror atop her vanity.

She was not beautiful.

She was too short.

Her hair was an unremarkable brown.

She liked to read, and much to her surprise, she liked to fill a home with the heady scent of holiday baking. She liked watching Pietr Sorenson work his ingenious kindness on this village, and she liked very much kissing him and sharing confidences with him.

She did not particularly like Lord Apollo. He exhibited charm when he wanted something, but had little else to recommend him and much to give a lady pause.

Pietr hoped that his decision to take the cathedral post had been an act of courage rather than an act of despair. Marrying Lord Apollo would be both. He had told Joy to expect a proposal at Christmas, *informed* her of her impending good fortune. She'd smiled and acted enormously pleased when all she'd been was enormously relieved.

Such a difference between those two emotions. A whole vast moor of difference.

The room across the corridor was silent. Pietr had apparently settled in to read his racy French novel or some Norse philosopher, maybe a little of both. Reading was a pleasure, but a solitary one. He had endured as a man apart for years, and Joy would still be a woman apart when she married Lord Apollo.

But she was not Lady Apollo yet. Before she lost her nerve, she rose, blew out the candle on the vanity, and crossed the chilly corridor. She did not knock. She simply slipped into Pietr's room.

"I have come a-viking," she said. "To steal a night with you all for myself."

He rose from the chair by the hearth. His room was not quite as warm as hers, but it was comfortable. He wore only a blue velvet dressing gown and pajama trousers, and his feet were clad in worn slippers.

He held a book in his hand, keeping his place with a finger between the pages. That boded ill for Joy's plans, as if he'd thank her kindly and just as kindly escort her back to her own bed, then resume his reading.

"I debated coming to you," he said. "I did not want to presume. I suspect in another quarter hour..."

Joy advanced toward him, intent on touching the bare flesh of his chest. "Yes?"

"In another quarter hour, I would have crawled across the corridor on my knees, prepared to beg. This is not wise, Joy."

"Yes, it is. To spend this night apart would be unwise."

He took her hand and pulled her near. "In the morning, we will have to live with the memories."

"At least I will have those." She kissed him, and yet, he remained unyielding. "Pietr, if you tell me to return to my own bed, to toss and turn all night, wishing and hoping, then I will do as you ask. I would much rather for once do as *I* please."

He set his book on the mantel. "As *we* please. I am not merely complicit in your desires, Joy. I am indulging my own as well. Are we clear on that?"

"Your vicarly conscience won't trouble you?"

"Vicars, let it be noted, are human. We have hearts and bodies and hopes. You are not spoken for. Neither am I. If you choose me for your own, for this one night, I am ecstatic to be claimed."

He'd worked out the theology of viking to his satisfaction, apparently, while for Joy, theology didn't come into it. *Seeing* herself, her needs, her desires, her wishes—and seeing Pietr—did.

"To bed with us, then," she said, resting against him. "Please, to bed, and for once, I am grateful that winter nights are so long."

He scooped her up in his arms and gently laid her on the turned-down quilts. "I will love you to exhaustion. I promise you that."

"How many times?"

He laughed, a low, naughty chortle. "I adore you, Joy Danforth. I will love you to exhaustion and revive you with my kisses. I will need reviving too." He unbelted his dressing gown and hung it on the bedpost. "Your dressing gown, Miss Danforth."

Ye gods, he was a fine specimen. All that shoveling, chopping, and marching about the village had honed him into magnificent fitness. His pajama trousers hung low on lean hips, and his...

Joy knelt up on the mattress and fumbled with the belt of her dressing gown. "What were you reading?"

"Nothing. I was staring at some book or other and thinking of you taking down your hair, undressing, *washing* just yards from where I sat aching and debating."

"I ache too, Pietr." Joy's heart ached, for as he'd said, tomorrow would come, and she would climb into a westbound coach to cross the moor. But now, her body ached, wonderfully. She was hot and needy and breathless while simply kneeling on the bed.

She passed him her dressing gown and situated herself under the covers. Pietr pinched out his reading candles, banked the fire, and joined her. The sensation of the mattress dipping, the piney scent of his soap, the book set aside on the mantel... All so domestic and precious.

"Promise me something," he said, slipping an arm around her shoulders. "Promise me you will not regret this, Joy. Promise me that you will be wildly self-indulgent with me, you will demand anything you please. Not simply ask, demand it of me."

She eased herself over him. "We will ask each other. No regrets, no holding back." She began her spree of wild self-indulgence—what an intriguing notion—by kissing Pietr's brow, then exploring the contours of his chest one caress at a time.

The rhythm of their lovemaking began slowly, reverently, with each taking turns. She explored his textures and tastes, he revealed to her the exquisite sensitivity of her own breasts. She listened to his heart and stroked his cheeks with the pads of her thumbs—he'd shaved just before bed, apparently—and he touched his tongue to the pulse beating at her throat.

By subtle degrees, Joy came out of hibernation. She set aside worries and schemes, she abandoned rules and reservations and purely delighted in the bounty Pietr set before her. By the time she was on her back, fifteen stone of Viking lover atop her, she had learned much and loved much.

"If you stop now, Pietr, you will break my heart."

"I'm savoring. The next part is..." He smoothed her hair back from her brow. "Holy, for want of a better word. Precious. Beyond precious."

He eased closer, and Joy guided him to her and rolled her hips. "There," she said. "Right there. Please."

He was an excruciatingly patient lover, which only made Joy all the more desperate. To be joined with him, to be as one flesh, inebriated every sense. His weight, his warmth, his strength, his mouth, his hands... She devoured the sensations until they gathered into a storm of pleasure that left her clinging to him and panting.

Her first coherent thought was that the poets had not lied after all, but even their words failed to convey the magnificence of Pietr Sorenson's loving desire.

"You cannot fall asleep after that mere opening gambit," he said, lips very near her ear. "When I said exhaustion, I meant exhaustion, Joy." He moved, and the result was another little shock of pleasure.

"A moment, please."

In this, too, he was generous, rearranging them so Joy was sprawled on his chest, the better to put her in charge of the next engagement.

Gambits, sorties, flourishes. She lost track of where one pleasure ebbed and another began, until she was floating on the edge of sleep in a bliss so profound as to defy description. Complete relaxation, utter peace, and transcendent bodily joy settled around her in Pietr's embrace.

"If this be exhaustion," she murmured, kissing him languidly, "then we have made the most of it."

He eased from her and, in a few lazy thrusts, spent on her belly. "Amen."

She did not recall him tidying up, other than a few gentle swipes of a cloth across her middle. Then she was wrapped in his arms and drifting toward oblivion.

How glad she was that she'd come to him. How glad she was that she'd seen the woman in the mirror as a person whose needs and wants mattered. How delighted she was that Pietr's needs and wants had mattered to him too.

She had not been entirely honest with him, though. She'd promised him that their night of loving would result in no regrets. She was already regretting that she would have to leave this bed, get into that westbound coach, and never again make love with Pietr Sorenson.

"JOHN COACHMAN, ATTEND ME." Pietr adopted his Wrath of

Yorkshire voice, which generally lost effectiveness on anybody over the age of six. Still, the blood of Vikings flowed through his veins, as did the blood of a Rothton pie-contest judge. More to the point, he was Joy Danforth's lover, however fleetingly.

John Coachman peered down at him from the box. "Aye, guv?"

"That's vicar to you. Pass me your flask."

A dented silver vessel was tossed down. "Fancy a nip?"

"I do not fancy a nip of the hog swill you have doubtless procured for your morning's work. Nor shall you overimbibe any further than you already have, though I'm well aware you likely have a second flask in your boot."

"Bloody cold in these parts, Your Reverence. If you don't mind my—"

"There is a lady present," Pietr snapped. "Mind your tongue. You have already proven your inability to navigate the local surrounds. I have given Miss Danforth a detailed map of your route. If she tells you to turn left, you turn left. If she tells you to halt and rest the horses because a hill approaches, you halt and rest the horses.

"That one,"—Pietr went on, gesturing with his chin toward Hiram—"is cargo, do you understand me? He can whine about needing to warm up, he can wheedle for you to dawdle with him in the various commons of the posting inns, and you will ignore him. You heed the lady, or it will go very hard for you. We have two dukes in this village, and they will think nothing of conveying their displeasure with you to any lowly marquess or his spare."

"Two dukes?"

"Walden has a temper, as is known the length and breadth of London. Rothhaven has never needed to so much as raise his voice to convey his ire. Heed the lady if you want to keep your post."

"Can I have me flask back?"

"Miss Danforth will return it to you when she has been safely delivered to her destination." Not before. Pietr had discussed this with Joy as dawn had approached, and she'd seen the wisdom of his precautionary measures.

The first post coach had come in from the west shortly before noon, and two stagecoaches had followed. Joy had tarried over her midday meal, then she'd sat at Pietr's desk watching the birds when she ought to have been penning a note to her mama. She'd towed Pietr up to his bedroom, there to kiss him farewell beneath a fading bunch of mistletoe.

And now she was leaving, as she must, and Pietr must let her go.

Hiram strutted about pigeon-fashion on the porch as if disdaining to allow good Yorkshire snow to touch his boots—the boots Pietr had polished for him—while Joy supervised the securing of the luggage at the back of the coach.

"All ready," she said, smiling at Hiram and motioning him down. "Mr. Sorenson, your hospitality has been the greatest kindness. I will always be in your debt."

"The pleasure was mine. Safe journey, Miss Danforth." They'd said their farewells in Pietr's bedroom, throughout the night, and again when weak winter light had slanted in the window. *With my body, I thee worship...* The words of the old wedding service had resonated through Pietr's heart and soul with every caress and kiss.

"I will miss you," Joy said quietly as Hiram minced down the steps, slapping his gloves against his thigh.

Pietr adjusted the scarf he'd given Joy so it lay more snugly about her ears. "I awoke this morning to a revelation, Joy Danforth. I have been lonely. I have rattled around in a house meant for a large family, and I have regretted the many empty rooms. I regret them no more. All the years of feeling set apart, all the nights of wondering, brought me to a moment when I was apart no longer. I have known soul-deep joy, and for that, I will always be fiercely grateful."

Her gaze went to the upper floors. "I am fiercely grateful too, Pietr. I will think of you often, and those will be lovely, lovely thoughts."

He kissed her cheek. He was allowed that much, and for an instant, he lingered near, then he straightened. This little drama was doubtless being witnessed from the innyard. If he wasn't mistaken,

Ned Wentworth was marching across the green, and it was time to get on with the parting.

"In you go," he said, flipping down the coach's steps. "Danforth, your sister is ready to depart. Comport yourself to her satisfaction, or I will bring down the retribution of the angels upon you."

Not that the heavenly host had ever taken orders from Pietr before.

Hiram approached the coach. "Vicar. Thanks for your hospitality. I will mind my sister."

"See that you do." Pietr handed Joy in and glowered down at Danforth. There was good in the young man, but it was fading fast under the weight of desperation and self-interest.

Danforth climbed into the coach. Pietr closed the door and stepped back, and then the coachy was yelling to the team, and Joy Danforth was trotting out of Pietr's life.

The ache was awful and sweet, miserable and precious. Time would help—a widower knew that much—and time would be the thief of dear, dear memories.

"Good riddance?" Ned Wentworth asked, sauntering across the street.

"I see you've learned how to wear a proper scarf. Good day, Wentworth." The coach took the turn that headed west and was lost from view.

"You watch that vehicle as if your hopes and dreams just struck out across the moor, Vicar. If you're that desperate for a cribbage opponent, I suppose I can oblige."

Pietr reached for patience, for humility, for compassion, and all he could touch was heartache. "Wentworth, have you something to say? I have a sermon to compose." A dream to mourn.

Though in truth, Pietr would sit and simply watch the birds. He'd watched the birds for years when he'd first arrived at Rothton. *Behold the birds of the heavens: for they sow not, neither do they reap, nor gather into barns; yet your heavenly Father feedeth them...*

Pietr had watched them, marveled at their industry, their beauty, and their energy.

"Yes, I have something to say," Ned Wentworth replied. "I usually do, if anybody will listen. The vestry committee is attempting to decorate the assembly rooms for this evening's do, and you are needed. Rothhaven and Walden will soon come to blows, and the duchesses said if matters reached a bad pass, I was to summon you as the nearest we have to a heavenly intercessor. Lady Althea said I was not to allow you to politely cozen me into leaving you to brood."

My heart is shattered, and life goes on. "This happens every year because Blackwell insists on plying the decorating committee with his Christmas punch, which is the only way Mrs. Blackwell will permit her husband to sample that punch before sundown. Tell them to hang mistletoe in every doorway and greenery at the windows. It's not complicated."

Wentworth studied him with a shrewd gaze. "Tried that. You can curse fate, shake your fist at God, and wrestle demons all you please, Vicar, but I'm to fetch you, so fetch you I shall. I have more experience than you can possibly dream of with wrestling both demons and dukes. *Come along.*"

Wentworth, may he suffer frostbite to his arrogance, spoke for not one but two duchesses, and for Lord Nathaniel's lady, whom Pietr accounted a friend. Then too, Wentworth's pleasant tone suggested he would enjoy physically pitting himself against a heartbroken vicar who had three inches of height and ten stone of misery on him.

"For the love of heaven," Pietr said, stalking along the path cut across the green, "why must I nanny a pair of dukes?"

"You nanny everybody, as best I can tell," Wentworth said, ambling along in his wake. "You said meddling goes with the job. Now I ask you to meddle, and you turn up crotchety. One would almost think you expected a lump of coal in your stocking."

"Hush before I pound you flat." Pietr stopped walking. "I apologize. I am out of sorts. Violence solves nothing."

"Whoever said that had no brothers."

Wentworth was amused, blast him.

He climbed the steps to the inn and unwound his scarf. "That no-violence fellow had no mates to pull him up short when he got out of line. No vicar to pummel his conscience when his decency wandered to far-off lands. An occasional pummeling can clear the air wonderfully where I come from. Besides, a fellow has a reputation to protect, and sometimes, that means putting up his fives."

"Where you come from," Pietr retorted, "the air savors of brimstone, and the children are left to starve in the street." He tromped up the inn's steps, the sound of raised voices drifting down from the assembly rooms.

"I'd say you're here just in the nick of time," Wentworth replied. "Before Rothhaven turned up epileptic, he was a normal boy with a normal pair of fists. I suspect he'd delight in smacking sense into Walden, and Walden wouldn't dare smack him back. Could be fun."

Their Graces were apparently arguing over the wisdom of hanging mistletoe in a doorway. Walden protested that such an arrangement would stop traffic. Rothhaven pointed out that the press of traffic would ensure nobody lingered overlong exchanging holiday kisses.

"Hang the perishing mistletoe in the doorways," Pietr nearly shouted, "and hang it in random locations. Near the punch bowls, but not at the punch bowls. By the dessert table, but not at the dessert table. From the central chandelier. Hang it most especially over where the wallflowers sit, and cease making such a disgraceful racket. The holidays are a joyous time."

Rothhaven, who rarely left the grounds of his ducal hall, exchanged a frown with his brother, Lord Nathaniel. "Have you been at the wassail, Sorenson?"

"Not yet, but I intend to remedy that oversight."

The two dukes, both substantial, dark-haired specimens not much given to smiling, seemed amused. Lord Nathaniel, for some reason, found it necessary to consult his pocket watch. Dody Wiles was grinning outright, and Tom Lumley was winking as if he had a splinter in his eye. Old Man Weller lifted a tankard—had somebody won a bet?—and Mr. Petrie held out a glass to Pietr.

"Woman trouble, lad?"

"Of course not." *And I am not a lad.* Pietr took the drink to be polite, but he knew better than to guzzle it. He wanted to, though. With every passing moment, Joy traveled farther away, and the notion made him wild.

"That's worse," Wiles said. "When you want to have woman trouble, but she's not having any of it. Heard the little miss was off to marry a lord."

"And what good can possibly come of that?" Ned Wentworth muttered, gesturing for Petrie to pour him a measure. "How could she give up *all this* for the blandishments of wealth and standing?"

All this was a pile of fragrant greenery, some bare tables, and a polished plank floor. A battered spinet sat in a corner, and chairs were stacked against the wall.

"Don't begrudge us our humble pleasures, Mr. Wentworth." The scolding note in Pietr's voice horrified him. Scolding vicars were a blight upon society.

"Will you miss these pleasures?" Rothhaven inquired ever so casually.

"Miss them?" Wiles asked. "Why should he miss them? God knows, this place don't change from year to year."

"Decade to decade," Mr. Weller muttered. "Century to century."

Walden ambled to the side of the room and hefted some chairs, setting them down in a circle. "What's amiss, Sorenson?"

Pietr went to the window rather than join the circle of men swilling ale and putting off the task at hand. In the distance, a coach and four trotted across a white canvas toward a distant horizon.

"Miss Danforth's departure has left me out of sorts. I enjoyed having company." Having a friend, a companion, a *lover.*

"Don't we all enjoy that sort of company?" Lord Nathaniel asked, to a round of hear, hears. "If Miss Danforth enjoyed your company, why let her go?"

"She deserves more than an assistant dean who never aspired to be a dean, much less a saint."

Rothhaven took him gently by the arm and steered him to a seat. "They don't know, Sorenson, because you haven't told them. Why is that, I wonder?"

Pietr sat. He did not want to sit. He wanted to run after the Danforth coach and demand that Joy marry him. Not Lord Appalling Bellingham. *Him*.

"I have accepted a post as assistant dean at one of the northern cathedrals. While I have enjoyed my years here, one wants to make a difference, to use one's talents where they will make a difference. I will leave shortly after the New Year."

Pietr expected congratulations. He expected inane toasts—the punch was quite good—and he expected platitudes. *We'll miss you. Best of luck. Our loss is the Church's gain.* Anything, but this fraught silence.

Though if cathedrals could boast of any gift in quantity, it was silence. Eternal, hallowed, chilling silence.

CHAPTER SEVEN

Hiram fidgeted with the capes of his greatcoat. He fidgeted with the lap robes. He put the shade down. He put the shade up, the better to glower out the window.

"Cargo." The word conveyed petulance and bewilderment. "Vicar called me cargo. Where does it say that a man of the cloth gets to wield such an insult against his betters with impunity?"

You are not better than Pietr Sorenson. "Are you still feeling under the weather, Hiram?"

"I am in the very pink, thank you. A man who cannot deal stoically with a passing affliction is no man at all."

Was it an affliction when the misery was caused by a flask—a flask already again in evidence—that the man pressed to his own lips? Or was the more accurate word *stupidity*?

"Did Lord Apollo give you that flask?"

Hiram smiled, the expression smug. "A consolation gift, he said. I'd lost a bit of coin to him, and he passed it over to console me. He's generous like that. Fine quality in a man."

His lordship was a show-off. He would pass over a little fashion accessory to the poor fool who'd just lost enough coin to buy that trinket ten times over. Lord Apollo would never go quietly from one elderly household to another, discreetly checking coal supplies and hauling water into kitchens. He would never teach children to skate so that parents had one less bother on winter mornings. He would never see that a lamed drover could become an expert carver. He would never organize a brigade of juvenile snow shovelers, nor think to send them home with a hot potato in each pocket.

"Generosity is a fine quality," Joy said. Generosity of time, energy, consideration. To toss aside an unneeded bauble for the sake of impressing a lot of inebriates was not generosity. "Hiram, do you aspire to be generous? What exactly are your aspirations?"

"To be the envy of my peers, of course. Marrying a Bellingham cousin would help with that, and some luck at the tables would not go amiss. Holiday house parties have seen more than one fellow's fortune made."

The coach navigated a wide curve, and for a moment, the village came into view in the distance. The spire of the church was a white lance against a blue sky, and the houses and shops clustered together as if having a cozy chat on a sunny morning.

"Damned glad to be rid of the place," Hiram muttered, saluting with his flask. "Rural busybodies are the worst busybodies, mark me on that, Joy. They have nothing better to do than gossip and tattle while they idle away their days half soused on the local brew. They turn up pious every Sunday so they can collect more slander in the churchyard."

Joy considered her younger brother, whose face was pale and puffy, whose flask remained in his hand. Hiram might have been describing the London gentlemen's clubs where he spent so much of his time. Full of gossip and tippling busybodies who nonetheless attended services regularly and even spared the occasional penny for the poor box.

"Why do you suppose I am encouraging Lord Apollo's suit, Hiram?"

He sent her a peevish look. "Because you ain't stupid." He

managed to imply the opposite. "You'll have all the furbelows and gewgaws you could ask for, a titled husband, and consequence with the people that matter."

"Are there people who do *not* matter, then?" To Pietr Sorenson, every soul in creation mattered, be they a duke or an urchin, be they a robin, a finch, or an egret.

"Yes, there are people who matter not at all, as you well know," Hiram retorted. "Unless you marry Lord Apollo, *we* will not matter, we Danforths, except as objects of pity and spite. Mama wants new frocks, and Papa has ideas for investments. I have an heiress to marry, some fine and not-too-distant day. I believe our stay in that execrable little cow byre of a village has addled your wits, Joy. The sooner you bring Lord Apollo up to scratch, the better for all."

The coach rounded the base of a hill, and the village disappeared from view.

"You know, Grandpapa tried to teach Papa how to run the import business."

Hiram sighed theatrically. "The best people eschew direct involvement in trade, Joy. They do not inflict it upon their children."

"Grandpapa was trying to inflict security and self-sufficiency on his son. Trying to show Papa a path toward bettering our prospects. Instead, we are the next thing to a charity case."

"No, we ain't. Not as long as Lord Apollo offers for you. Mama will have her dresses, and the creditors will learn some patience. I will meet all the right people and be set for life."

The Yorkshire sun on the vast expanse of snow was nearly blinding, as was the truth: Hiram, once a sweet, considerate boy, would be *ruined* for life if Joy married Lord Apollo. Hiram would disdain honest work. He would never care for anybody but himself and his cronies. He would pickle his liver and gamble away all the pretty flasks that tumbled into his lap.

"I love you, Hiram. You are my only sibling, my brother, and I have loved you since the day you came squalling into the world."

He grinned and tipped up his flask. "You ain't so bad yourself, most days. More to the point, Lord Apollo fancies you. That makes you the best of sisters, for now."

Though Hiram was not the best of brothers. Somehow, he had become arrogant, greedy, slothful, mean, and selfish. His gifts had been squandered, and he was facing a ruin far more dire than a simple want of coin.

"I do love you, Hiram, and I love Mama and Papa too." She rose and opened the slot that allowed communication with the coachman. "Stop the horses. We need to turn around. Now."

Hiram elbowed her back into her seat. "Drive on, you lackwit," he shouted. "She's naught but a female suffering a fit of the vapors."

"Stop the coach. Turn the horses around," Joy called. "And do it now."

The coach careened onward, and Hiram continued bellowing.

THE SILENCE in the assembly room stretched like ice over a birdbath, brittle and bright.

"Want to make a difference, do ye, Parson?" Wiles mused.

"I judge pie contests," Pietr said. "I feed birds. I have an entire shelf of Mrs. Peabody's remedies because she has to test them out on somebody, and I have the constitution of an ox. What sort of life can I offer a woman whose family depends upon her to make a decent match?"

"Lad," Mr. Petrie said, "ye be daft. Wiles here was drinking himself to death until you happened by with a request that he whittle you some birds for the children in the Sunday school. Next thing we know, the nippers are memorizing Scripture at a great rate to earn their birds, and Wiles has a few coins."

"Two years on," Mr. Wiles said, "I have more orders than I can handle. My children have a trade, and my missus isn't looking scared and cold all the time. Ye made a difference, Vicar."

"Biddy Peabody was half daft herself," Mr. Lumley said, "and then you tell her that her chamomile tea is the best you've had. She sends some to a cousin in York, who's willing to sell it in her shop, along with the other vile concoctions old Biddy stirs up. Biddy don't really need the coin, but now she's an expert on tisanes. A woman like our Biddy needs to be an expert on something, or she gets to being an expert on *us*."

What was Pietr to say to that? "Biddy has great compassion, but she's plagued by fears. Mixing up tonics gives her a way to deal with both."

"And what of my fears?" Lord Nathaniel said. "I lived for nearly five years without so much as attending an assembly, Sorenson, but I had one place I knew I could always go. One ear I could fill with my frustrations and dreams. You never turned me away, you were never too busy to share a drink or a game of chess. Week after week, I lived for just two hours of intelligent conversation or village gossip. Unlike our dear Biddy's potions, your tonics were always effective. I went back to the Hall a little less frantic and burdened. You made a difference."

An odd feeling was welling past the heartache of Joy's departure. "We are to be kind to one another. I enjoyed those games too, my lord."

"And when I no longer needed them," Lord Nathaniel replied, "you wished me well and fed your birds. When my darling Althea sought introductions in York to start her circulating schools among the poor, you politely battered down the door to every charitable association in the city and gently bludgeoned your bishop into supporting her work."

He held up a hand when Pietr would have interrupted.

"Then," his lordship went on, "you escorted her ladyship to meet with the *archbishop,* because you knew that his support would be a better endorsement than heaven's seal. Hundreds of poor children are now reading because of you, Sorenson. You made a difference."

Lady Althea—Lady Nathaniel now—had been determined, but

without a means of implementing her ideas. "She asked for my help," Pietr said. "It was little enough to do when the need is so great."

"And yet," His Grace of Walden said, "my sister did not come to me for help. She did not come to the family duke, the man who owns one of the largest banks in York. She came to the man who excels at making a difference."

Lumley took a philosophical sip of his wassail. "Missus and I get overwhelmed. So many weans and not enough coin. Then you find a way for them to earn a few pennies with the shoveling or weeding or sweeping. It's not charity. It's teaching them that hard work deserves a fair wage. That's all they need, some pride and ingenuity. We forget that."

He exchanged a look with Wiles. "Then you come around," Lumley went on, "reminding us that our brood is prodigious healthy. That our oldest has a talent for drawing—you've helped us see that, helped him hone that talent with Her Grace."

He peered at his drink. "You pointed out that wee Mary is clever with her letters. Missus and I forget those things, and yet, they matter, Vicar. Good health, a sound mind, some skills... They matter more than all the fancy coaches in the world. You not only remind us of that with words, you live that. You make a difference in your example. We don't want a vicar who spouts the Scriptures and can't be bothered to admire yet another new baby. We need you."

"I knit," Old Man Weller said, "because you reminded me that Mrs. Lumley hasn't the time, and her babies need blankets just the same. We have a lending library because of you, and don't the ladies just love to gather there and sort out the ills of the world? We have flowers on the green, free to anybody, because you prodded His Grace into providing the wherewithal. Go to your cathedral if you must, Vicar, but we will mourn the loss of you."

You have built a cathedral here. Joy had said that.

"Lest I be castigated for slacking," Rothhaven said, "I will entrust you and these good fellows with a little tale. Once upon a time, there was a man who suffered the falling sickness. The damned illness, and the measures taken to contain it, had turned him up flighty and fear-ful. He never ventured forth, never mixed with society. He was lonely as only a fool on the moor can be lonely."

"You were not a fool," Lord Nathaniel interjected.

"This is my tale," Rothhaven retorted. "I will tell it as I see fit."

"Brothers," Mr. Wentworth murmured.

"Go on," Pietr said, though he had the sense these offerings—for that's what they were—were somehow his confession. His tale.

"I had—the fellow, rather—had a ferociously bad seizure. The local vicar was called in to administer last rites. I was—the fellow, rather—was horrified. He'd not seen a strange face for years. He'd not had to make conversation, much less explain himself to anybody. Vicars are busybodies. They gossip and judge. They are a tolerated imposition on the people because the Crown's control of us must be bolstered by threats of eternal hellfire. Nobody needs a perishing vicar sticking his beak where it's not needed."

Precisely. "And that—"

Rothhaven held up a hand much as his brother had, and Pietr did not dare speak.

"I needed *that* vicar. Do you know what he did? That vicar, an unprepossessing fellow with the dimensions of a dragoon, asked me of my illness. 'Is it very difficult?' he asked. An hour later, I was still searching for words, still trying to explain myself to this patient fellow with the kind eyes, who pretended that lukewarm tea was ambrosia and stale shortbread manna from heaven. He simply *talked* to me. Asked the occasional question, and when he rose to leave..."

Rothhaven stared off at nothing, and the silence in the room spoke loudly of courage and hope.

"I did not want him to go," Rothhaven said. "I, who feared ridicule, who feared the next seizure, who feared *open windows*, did not want that man to leave me. I had spent time with a stranger, more than an hour. I had *taken tea with a caller.* I had held a conversation even. My entire view of myself—a hopeless eccentric doomed to soli-tude, a burden on my family—changed because a man stopped by for tea. You thanked me for the damned tea and made it convincing. You might have said a few prayers, but mostly, Pietr Sorenson, you listened, and you did not judge. Nathaniel rescued me from the madhouse, but my recovery did not truly start until you came to call."

Pietr set down his drink. He recalled that summons to the Hall, recalled expecting to find Lord Nathaniel in difficulties, only to find a very different situation indeed.

"You never betrayed our confidences," Lord Nathaniel said. "Never breathed a word, never questioned me about any of it. You have no idea, Sorenson, no earthly, heavenly, human idea of the difference you've made. How dare you abandon us now for some pile of pious old stones?"

"When my duchess and I needed a swift, discreet wedding ceremony," Rothhaven said, "we knew we could ask it of you. We knew you would safeguard our happiness, no questions asked."

"You and Her Grace were so obviously besotted," Pietr replied. "Utterly smitten. Of course you needed marrying." He looked around at a half-dozen men who regarded him solemnly in return. "I meddle... I have a license to meddle."

Ned Wentworth, who'd been noticeably quiet, remained by the window. "I wish to Almighty God somebody had been around to meddle on behalf of me and my family, Sorenson. Instead, it was Newgate, starvation, and crime until my path crossed Walden's. I suspect these men could recite your accomplishments until sundown, but the person you need to convince to stay here in Rothton isn't Pietr Sorenson, it's Pietr Sorenson's prospective wife."

"Joy must marry well," Pietr said. "I cannot change that."

"She could marry no finer man than you," Rothhaven said gently.

"Her family's situation is becoming known," Walden added. "She could marry Fat George himself, and that would not stop the creditors from seeking payment."

"Bellingham will wash his hands of them," Mr. Wentworth said, "even if he marries Miss Danforth. I manage His Grace's banks, and I know how Society politely turns its back on those who falter. Do you really want Miss Danforth to have to watch while his lordship cuts her off from the family that means so much to her?"

"I don't have the coin they need to come right," Pietr said. "Bellingham won't allow his in-laws to be cast into debtors' prison. I have room at the vicarage for them. I have my investments. My wife would never know hardship, but as for the rest of it... I cannot solve problems of that magnitude."

Mr. Wentworth sent a glower over his shoulder at the pair of dukes whom most of Society spoke of in whispers.

"Happens I know a banker with some blunt," Mr. Wentworth said. "He knows a couple of worthless idlers who excel at sorting out investments and finances. If that pair cannot bring order to the Danforth situation, then it cannot be done this side of heaven."

"I could not impose to that extent," Pietr said. Though, would Joy want him to impose? Did she *need* him to impose? To seek that kind of help? Humility was a virtue, wasn't it?

"The duchesses and my wife," Lord Nathaniel said, "would deal with us severely if we allowed all of your kindness and consideration to go unrepaid. You have a wealth of coin of the heart. We have an abundance of a different sort of resource. The Danforths can be taught to economize. They can be made to understand a ledger, just as we in the village have learned to be kind and honorable with one another."

Ned Wentworth turned to face the room and speared Pietr with a look. "I never wanted to be a pickpocket. Do you want to be a dean?"

A *pickpocket*? If Ned Wentworth could go from pickpocket to banker... Miracles were possible. Pietr had always believed that miracles were possible. Spring was a miracle, birds, healthy children, and human kindness. Most of all, human kindness was a miracle.

"No," Pietr said, getting to his feet. "No, I do not want to be a dean. Not ever. I do not want to leave Rothton, and I most assuredly do not want to spend the next twenty years wishing I had mustered the courage to offer for the woman I love."

Pietr's gelding would not be able to catch the coach, but he'd cross the moors safely enough. "Gentlemen, I leave you to your deco-rating. I have a declaration to make."

"Told ye," Wiles said. "My money's been on ye from the start, Vicar. Best of luck, but we'll all want to attend the wedding."

"Take Loki," Lord Nathaniel said. "He loves a good gallop, and he delights in snow."

"As do I." Pietr bowed to everybody at once and left at a smart but dignified march.

"STOP THE PERISHING COACH," Joy hollered over Hiram's bleatings. "Stop the coach this instant, or I will toss my brother into the snow!"

She was determined enough to do it too. Not angry, or not very angry, but determined. Grandpapa had meant well, meant to offer his son better prospects than Grandpapa himself had faced, but those intentions had been misguided.

"No place to turn the 'orses," came back from the box. "Nothing but damned moor."

And yet, the coach slowed. The coach finally slowed. The ground-eating trot became a jarring jog, and then the horses ambled to a halt.

"We got us a highwayman," the coachy yelled. "One bloke, but on a damned fast horse. No point risking the beasts on this footing."

The bend in the road allowed Joy to see a lone rider streaking along in the coach's wake.

"Fine riding," Hiram said. "A madman, clearly, but he can ride that hell beast."

The rider's scarf streamed out behind him, his head was bare, and the wind had turned his cheeks ruddy.

"That is no madman," Joy said. "That is my Viking."

"Vicar, you mean. Did you forget a locket or something back at the parsonage?"

"Not a locket, but something precious." *I left behind my heart.*

The horse pranced up to the coach, a great dark steed who did not appear to notice that the moor was covered in snow. Joy opened the door the better to lean out and see Pietr stop his mount directly before the team.

"You want I should stand and deliver?" the coachy asked. "All I have is me spare flask. Ye done already nicked my good one."

"I want you to cease nattering so I can cast my heart into the lady's keeping." Pietr nudged the horse around to the side of the coach, which put him only slightly above Joy's eye level. "I apologize for interrupting your journey, Miss Danforth."

"I am delighted that you interrupted my journey. You cut quite a dash on that horse, Mr. Sorenson."

"A *dash*? I do?" He petted the horse, whose sides heaved with exertion. "Loki is a good lad. Likes a run every now and then, for which God be thanked."

"I have realized something," Joy said, rather than risk that the words would go unsaid. "Something important."

"As have I. Ladies first."

"If I marry Lord Apollo, I am ensuring my brother's ruin. My family's ruin. Money must be dealt with, render unto Caesar and all that, but Hiram is turning rancid before my eyes. Another year or two of strutting around in finery he cannot afford, and he will be lost to all hope. The only reason Lord Apollo has decided to marry me is that I'm short and plain."

"The blighter *told* you that?"

The horse's ears pricked at Pietr's tone.

"Yes. His lordship is short. What he lacks in inches, he makes up for in arrogance. He *likes* looking down on me. Likes that I will always be grateful for his proposal. He said he will have no trouble managing me and that his good looks will be enough to ensure that our children are handsome. I am to be grateful and dainty. I am not dainty, Pietr. I am little and fierce."

"You and yonder vicar are daft," Hiram said. "The pair of you are flaming—"

"Hush." Joy and Pietr had spoken in unison.

"Be still," Pietr added. "I must be heard, or I will go daft in truth. Joy Danforth, I have only modest means, though they are adequate. I am accounted a fine judge of pies, my toes are made of cast iron from having been tromped on by so many wallflowers and by the estimable Mrs. Blackwell. I am not given to long sermons nor to chattering, except apparently when I am proposing."

He took up the reins, though the horse was standing as docilely as a lamb. "My heart is yours," Pietr said, regarding Joy with blue, blue eyes. "Will you have the rest of me as well? Please say yes. Your family can live with us if need be—we have room at the vicarage— and my guardian angels have agreed to sort out all the money and whatnot. Lord Apollo does not deserve you, and—I mean this in all humility—you have done nothing to deserve the penance he would be either."

Pietr sat very tall on his horse, the chilly breeze riffling his hair. Hiram had fallen silent, while the coachy was dabbing at his eyes with his sleeve.

"Pietr Sorenson," Joy said, "you have a genius for kindness as wide and magnificent as the moors. You have a soul as lovely as the blue Yorkshire heavens, and you are the warmth at the heart of an entire village. You are the love of my life, and I will speak my vows with you and only with you."

"You mean that?" he asked. "You will marry me?"

He was so hopeful, so brave. "Yes, I will marry you, and that old cathedral will just have to muddle on without you. We will build our own edifice out of gratitude, kindness, caring, and laughter."

"And pleasure," he added softly. "Profound pleasure."

"That too, but the foundation will be love, Pietr."

"Amen. The foundation will be love."

The coachy flourished a dented flask. "I'll drink to that. Don't suppose there's someplace I can turn these 'orses about? Gettin' a might nippy up here with all this proposin' and plightin' goin' on."

"Danforth," Pietr called. "Can you manage to stay in the saddle all the way back to the village? Loki has galloped off the fidgets, and Joy and I have more to say to each other."

"Do go on, Hiram," Joy said, stepping back from the coach's door. "You fancy yourself a man of accomplishments. Get that horse back to the village in one piece, why don't you?"

Loki chose then to start propping and prancing in the snow, which seemed to amuse Pietr. "He's a good lad, Danforth. Just a bit lively. Wants encouragement and guidance."

Hiram watched the horse curvetting and fussing. "P'raps I'll just ride up top?"

"Very well," Pietr said, climbing from the saddle. "Loki, you can toddle along behind the coach." He fixed the reins to the boot. "John Coachman, you'll reach a crossroads on the other side of this hill, and you can turn the team there. Danforth, out of that coach and take my scarf. You'll need it."

Hiram got down, Pietr climbed in, and a few minutes later, Joy was rolling along, snuggled next to the man she loved.

"What changed your mind?" she asked. "You let me start across the moor, Pietr, and every bend in the road only broke off another piece of my heart."

"I conferred with wiser heads," Pietr said, looping an arm around Joy's shoulders. "I cannot abandon the place where I am most useful and where I so clearly thrive. I needed to be shown a few home truths, and I need you to thrive beside me. What changed your mind?"

Oh, to be next to him again, to be cuddled right up next to him. "How do you know I did change my mind?"

"The coach was slowing down as I rode up. I left strict instructions that the coachman was to listen only to you. You told him to halt. Why?"

"Because, Hiram was yawping about the right people, and luck at the tables, and new dresses... all the things that brought the Danforths to a sorry pass in the first place. I saw that if I did not take the steps with my family that my grandfather had declined to take— to see that they lived within their means, to remind them that new slippers must be paid for—then we would be not merely in debt, but ruined as human beings. I might mean well, marrying Lord Apollo, but I'd been fooling myself about what the actual results would be and about what love required of me."

"The Danforths won't be ruined," Pietr said, arranging the robe over both their laps. "They will practice economies, liquidate assets, and live humbly, but they won't be ruined. Mr. Wentworth has sent his dukes into action, and that's all that need be said on the matter. I must kiss you now."

Pietr in fact kissed her all the way back to the village, a shorter distance than Joy would have preferred. The coachy pulled up at the inn where, for some reason, a crowd had assembled.

"I assume," a tall, dark-haired fellow said as Joy climbed from the coach, "that you have restored our vicar to his usual good spirits, Miss Danforth?"

Pietr descended and took Joy's hand. "His Grace of Walden bids you good morning, Joy. His Grace of Rothhaven will do likewise in a moment. I am happy to announce that Miss Danforth has restored my fine spirits to a full measure of holiday good cheer. She has agreed to marry me, and we will make our home here for as long as children need skating lessons and new babies need blankets."

"A very long time indeed," Walden said, bowing to Joy. "Congrat-ulations, best wishes. Wassail for all, to celebrate the happy occasion!"

A stampede ensued, one that left even Mrs. Blackwell smiling. Hiram joined the throng, as did the coachman, various elders, more than a few children, and the rest of the village. The holiday assembly began as a spontaneous celebration and continued well past dark.

A new tradition began, of holding the holiday assembly at an earlier hour, the better to include the whole village. Other traditions remained—the skating lessons, the snow shoveling and flower patches —and new souls arrived, including several little darlings born at the vicarage.

Whether the undertaking was building a family, maintaining a village, or planting some posies, as long as Pietr and Joy dwelled at the vicarage, the foundation was love.

The foundation was always, always love.

TO MY DEAR READERS

I do love me a holiday tale! There's just something special about a bleak time of year being when many of us form some of our sweetest memories and reconnect with our dearest friends. I am left wondering, though, about what Ned Wentworth, now all grown up and sporting about in London finery, will do for his own happily ever after.

Clearly, Ned has waited long enough to be rescued from the moor, or the City, or whatever lonely wilderness he's inhabiting these days. Fortunately for him, Lady Rosalind Kinwood has need of a gentleman's assistance. Ned doesn't quite consider himself a gentleman—Newgate, felony charges, and so forth—but he isn't about to leave Lady Rosalind to investigate a dangerous situation on her own.

I've included an excerpt below from *Never a Duke*, which is scheduled for publication this spring. This will be book seven of the *Rogues to Riches*, and—as far as I know—the series finale.

I've also included an excerpt from my next **Mischief in Mayfair** title, *Miss Dignified*, which comes out in January 2022. (Web store and library release Dec. 14.) This story features Captain

Dylan Powell, self-appointed guardian angel of former soldiers down on their luck in London, and Mrs. Lydia Lovelace, Dylan's housekeeper. She's making his house into a home, and he's making her question the very loyalties that drove her to London in the first place. Here, there be smoochin'!

To keep up with my new releases, discounts, and preorders, you can follow me on **BookBub**. If you'd like a little more of the backstories and out-takes, I send off a **newsletter** about once a month. I will never spam you or sell, give away, or trade your email addy, and unsubscribing is easy. I also have a **Deals** page on my website if you want to see what's been discounted in the **web store**, or which titles are scheduled for early release in the store.

However you choose to keep in touch, I wish you, as always, happy reading!

Grace Burrowes

Read on for an excerpt from **_Never a Duke_**!

NEVER A DUKE—EXCERPT

Lady Rosalind Kinwood's maid has gone missing, and nobody, not her titled father, not her brothers, not her companion, will help Rosalind discover what has become of the young lady. Rosalind turns to the vaguely scandalous Ned Wentworth for assistance...

The problem with Ned Wentworth was his eyes.

Rosalind came to that conclusion as she pretended to browse a biography of a long-dead monarch. She had come to the bookstore early, the better to ensure that her companion, Mrs. Beverly Barnstable, was thoroughly engrossed in the travelogues two floors above the biographies.

Ned Wentworth dressed with a gentleman's exquisite sense of fashion. He spoke and comported himself with a gentleman's faultless manners.

But his eyes did not gaze out upon the world with a gentleman's condescending detachment. Rosalind's brothers, by contrast, had by the age of eight learned how to glance, peruse, peer, and otherwise take only a casual visual inventory of life and to then pretend that nothing very interesting or important graced the scene.

Certainly nothing as interesting or important as her brothers themselves.

Ned Wentworth *looked* and he *saw*. His visual appraisals were frank and thorough, as if everything before him, from Rosalind's reticule, to a swan gliding across the Serpentine's placid surface, was simply a ledger that wanted tallying.

His eyes were a soft, mink brown, his hair the same color as Rosalind's. On him, the hue was sable, of a piece with his watchful gaze and sober attire. On her, the color was lamentably plain, according to Aunt Ida. He was on the tall side, but not a towering specimen like the Duke of Walden and not a fashionable dandy like the duke's younger brother.

Ned Wentworth's eyes said he'd somehow held out against domestication, unlike his adopted family, who had famously come from lowly origins to occupy a very high station. He prowled through life with a wild creature's confidence and vigilance, even as he partnered wellborn ladies through quadrilles and met their papas for supper in the clubs.

"She was quite the schemer, wasn't she?"

Rosalind turned to behold those serious brown eyes gazing at her. Up close, Ned Wentworth was a sartorial tribute to understated elegance. His attire had no flourishes—no flashy cravat pin, no excessive lace, no jewels in the handle of his walking stick.

His scent was similarly subtle, a hint of flower-strewn meadows, a whisper of cedar. Rosalind hadn't heard his approach, but she'd be able to identify him by scent in pitch darkness.

"Queen Elizabeth was devious," Rosalind replied, "but she died a peaceful death after nearly achieving her three score and ten. We must account her a successful schemer."

"Are you a successful schemer, my lady?"

Rosalind replaced the book on the shelf. "Do *you* attempt to flirt with me, Mr. Wentworth?"

The biographies were unpopular, hence the conversation was not overheard. Ned Wentworth had likely known that would be the case.

"If I were attempting to flirt with you," he said, "you'd likely cosh me over the head with yonder tome. Tell me about Miss Arbuckle."

Rosalind withdrew a folded sketch from her reticule. "A likeness. I am no portraitist, but Francine Arbuckle was willing to serve as my model on many occasions. She has no family in London, and the last I saw of her, my companion had sent her to retrieve a pair of dancing slippers from a shop near Piccadilly."

"Specifics, please. What shop?"

Rosalind endured an interrogation, and Mr. Wentworth's methodical inquiry helped her sort recollection from conjecture.

"I tried talking to the crossing sweepers," she said, when she'd recounted all she could remember regarding Arbuckle's disappearance. "They acted as if conversing with me would turn them to stone."

"They might have had trouble understanding you, my lady. They know their Cockney and cant and can recite you bawdy poems without number, but drawing-room elocution eludes them."

Rosalind had never considered that her speech might be incomprehensible. "Elocution eluded me for years as well. I developed a stammer after my mother's death. My governess was horrified." Rosalind was horrified. She never alluded to her stammer, while her brothers never let her forget it.

Mr. Wentworth frowned. "You stammered?"

"For years. My brothers teased me unmercifully. Then my aunt hired a Welshwoman as my drawing master, and she taught me to think of speaking as *recitativo*. I do not stammer when I sing, and if I can hear a melody..." Rosalind fell silent, for she was prattling. This was Ned Wentworth's fault, because after he posed a question, he *listened* to the lady's answer, and the whole time, he gazed at her as if her words mattered. Very bad of him. "This isn't helping us to find Arbuckle."

"Your secret is safe with me." He chose a book at random from the shelves. "Bankers learn more secrets than I ever aspired to know. We keep them close or soon go out of business."

He made a handsome picture, leafing through the book. Rosalind would like to sketch him thus, not that his appearance mattered one whit. "What sort of secrets?"

He turned a page. "Who has set up a discreet trust fund for a supposed godchild. Who is one Season away from ruin. Who has abruptly changed solicitors, such as might happen when the first firm is unwilling to suborn a bit of perjury or sharp practice."

Polite society kept Ned Wentworth at a slight distance, and Rosalind had always attributed that lack of welcome to his past. He was rumored to have met His Grace of Walden during the duke's little misunderstanding with the authorities, the little misunderstanding that had landed His Grace on a Newgate scaffold with a noose about his neck. His Grace had been merely Mr. Quinton Wentworth at the time and appallingly wealthy.

He was even wealthier now, but still Ned Wentworth's past did not recommend him to the matchmakers. Neither, apparently, did his present. "No wonder they are all afraid of you. You could ruin the lot of them."

He turned another page. "You are not afraid of me."

They were wandering far afield from the topic of Arbuckle's disappearance, and Rosalind had more information to convey. And yet, to *converse* with Mr. Wentworth was interesting. With men, she was usually reduced to argument, lecture, small talk, or exhortation. That she gave as good as she got in each category only seemed to make the situation worse.

"Why would I be afraid of you?" Rosalind said. "You are a gentleman, and you have agreed to help me."

He closed the book. "Your oldest brother is habitually in dun territory, Lady Rosalind, and your younger brother is barely managing on a generous allowance, very likely because he's trying to keep the firstborn son and heir out of the sponging house. I thought you should know this before I undertake a search for Miss Arbuckle."

The words made sense, but they were rendered in such polite, unassuming tones that Rosalind needed a moment to find the meaning in them.

"Do you expect me to pay you?" Rosalind had some ready cash, because wasting coin on fripperies was beyond her, and Papa had little clue what it cost to clothe a lady, much less run his own household.

"Of course not." Mr. Wentworth shoved the book back onto the shelf. "If your family is short of coin, then the sooner I put your mind at ease regarding remuneration for my efforts, the less likely you are to fret."

Fret? Whatever was he getting at? "You are being too delicate for my feeble female brain, Mr. Wentworth. Plain speech would be appreciated."

He selected another book, as casually as if he truly were browsing the biographies. "You promised in your note that if I heeded your summons, you would make it worth my while. A simple request for aid would have sufficed, my lady. You need not coerce me with coin."

Ah, well, then. His pride was offended. Having two brothers, Rosalind should have recognized the symptoms.

"I meant to trade favors, Mr. Wentworth. You have agreed to search for Arbuckle, and thus I will share with you the fact that Clotilda Cadwallader is considering allowing you to court her. She's said to be worth ten thousand a year."

The book snapped closed. "She's *what*?"

"Said to be worth—"

He shook his head. "I know to the penny what she's worth, and it's not ten thousand a year. What else can you tell me?"

"She might allow you to pay her your addresses." Rosalind offered this news with all good cheer, though Clotilda was a ninny-hammer. Men seemed to prefer ninnyhammers, alas. "You'd have to change your name to Cadwallader, but she says you aren't bad look-ing, you're solvent, and you would not be overly bothersome about filling the nursery." More delicate than that, Rosalind could not be.

"Because I have no title and need neither heir nor spare, and what married couple would ever seek one another's intimate company for any reason other than duty?"

Mr. Wentworth's tone presaged not affront, but rather, amusement—and bitterness.

"I know little of what motivates people to marry, and as for intimate company..." Too late, Rosalind realized that she'd sailed into an ambush of her own making.

"Yes, my lady?" The amusement had reached Mr. Wentworth's eyes. He was silently laughing at her, which merited a good Storming Off in High Dudgeon, except that his gaze held only a friendly sense of fun and nothing of mockery.

He was *teasing* her. Rosalind's brothers had teased her, before a mere sister had slipped beneath their notice. Arbuckle had occasionally teased her. But when Ned Wentworth teased, his watchful, noticing eyes warmed to a startling degree. A smile lurked in the subtle curve of his mouth, and the corners of his eyes crinkled.

I must sketch him thus, must catch that near smile. "We will now change the subject," Rosalind said, "because the alternative is to admit that I've mortified myself."

"Must we change the subject just as the conversation is becoming interesting?"

"You are twitting me." Or perhaps he was flirting with her? Not likely, but Rosalind had so little experience with flirtation she could forgive herself for wondering.

"On the basis of vast *in*experience, you were preparing to lecture me about your complete indifference to marital joy. Of course I was teasing you. And as for Miss Cadwallader... You will please inform her that I want a very large family."

"Do you?"

He put the book atop the shelf. "If Miss Cadwallader asks, you may assure her I do." His smile had gone from a subdued curving of the lips to a buccaneer's grin.

To blazes with sketching him. When Ned Wentworth smiled like that, Rosalind wanted to kiss him.

Order your copy of **Never a Duke**, and read on for an excerpt from **Miss Dignified**!

MISS DIGNIFIED—EXCERPT

Chapter One

"That is a kitten." The audacious little beast—a calico—batted at the toe of Captain Dylan Powell's boot as if to herd him out of his own kitchen. "I do not recall giving permission to add another dependent to my household."

If asked, he would have refused. Half of London's disabled and unemployed soldiers already relied on Dylan's hospitality, and that was quite challenging enough.

"That," Mrs. Lydia Lovelace retorted, "is a pantry mouser, and you, Captain Powell, are intruding belowstairs unannounced again. We have discussed this. If you're peckish, you may ring for a tray and I will happily oblige you." In the dim light of the kitchen hearth, she gathered her shawl in a manner that conveyed vexation—with him.

"It's nearly midnight," Dylan replied. "I would not trouble you over bread and cheese."

"Bread and cheese." Mrs. Lovelace swished past him to the window box. "You hare about London at all hours, on foot, *in this weather*, and think to subsist on bread and cheese." She tossed the longer tail of her shawl over one shoulder with all the panache of a

Cossack preparing to gallop across the snowy steppes. "I should let you starve, but then I'd be in need of a post."

While the kitten pounced on Dylan's boots, then pronked away with its back arched, Mrs. Lovelace put together an omelet of ham, cheese, and bacon. At the same time, she had a rack of toast browning over the coals, and a kettle on to boil.

For Dylan to sit, even on the hard chair before the kitchen table, was to fall prey to a staggering weight of fatigue. By a London gentleman's standards, midnight was not late. By a soldier's standards, midnight was hours past bedtime. Though he'd sold his commission years ago, Dylan's body had never lost the habit of the soldier's hours.

He rose to turn the toast—when had his hips acquired the aches of an eighty-year-old man?—and the kitten scampered after him. Rather than risk stepping on such a small pest, he scooped the beast up.

"Does it have a name?" he asked. The feline squeezed its eyes closed and commenced rumbling. *I'm surrounded by insubordination.*

"She. Calicoes are always female in my experience, and no, she does not. Not yet."

Dylan resumed his seat as the kitchen filled with the scents of good, simple food. "Because you think I'd turn her out?"

Mrs. Lovelace sent him an eloquently skeptical glance. "Even you would not turn away a kitten on such a foul night."

No, he would not, but come morning...

"It's merely raining." Dylan had marched through worse and barely noticed the wet, but this rain was London rain, which could turn to sleet at any season of the year. Welsh rain was well behaved by comparison, usually more of a pattering mist, and often bringing rainbows in its wake.

Thoughts of Wales were never cheering, and never far from his mind.

"Rain with a bitter wind," Mrs. Lovelace retorted, taking the toasting rack off the hearth. She opened the rack and began spreading butter over the warm slices. "River fog reeking of foul miasmas. Footpads on every corner. That you have not succumbed to brain fever or fallen prey to violence surely qualifies as miraculous."

"Would you miss me?" The question slipped out, not quite teasing. Perhaps Mrs. Lovelace was right—she was frequently right, also somewhat less than respectful of her employer. The late hour, an empty belly, and the dirty weather had taken a toll on Dylan's wits.

"I would miss my post." She cut the buttered toast into triangles and arranged it on a plate with the steaming omelet. "You should wash your hands, sir."

Now she gave him orders, albeit couched as a suggestion and served with a side of scowling disapproval. To wash his hands, Dylan would have to stand again, and now that he was finally home and parked on his arse, even crossing the kitchen loomed like a three-day forced march.

He nonetheless set the kitten on the warm bricks of the raised hearth and went to the wet sink to do as he was told. Junior officers in particular learned to do as they were told, though half the time the result was death or disgrace—at least when the orders came from Colonel Aloysius Dunacre.

"Will you join me?" Dylan asked, returning to the table. Mrs. Loveless had made a prodigious amount of food, more than he could comfortably eat at one sitting.

"I'll see to the tea."

The kitten curled up in a basket on the hearth, looking small and vulnerable all on its lonesome, also contented and sweet, damn it.

Dylan stared at the hot food, an unexpected comfort on an otherwise frustrating night. "For what I am about to receive, I am abjectly grateful. Please do sit, Mrs. Lovelace." He cast around for a means of inducing her to get off her feet. "To have you racketing about will ruin my digestion."

She wore no cap at this late hour, and Mrs. Lovelace did set great store by her caps. She set great store by feather dusters, recipes for lifting stains, and medicinals for every occasion. Dylan had never met a woman so ferociously competent at domesticity, nor so ruthless in her warfare against dirt and disorder.

She brought the tea tray to the table and sat across from him, perched on the very edge of her chair. "The eggs might need salt."

Dylan portioned off a third of the omelet and set it on a saucer. "Try it for yourself. I cannot possibly finish this and good food ought not to go to waste." He pushed the plate over to her, then added a triangle of toast. Challenging Mrs. Lovelace to bend a rule was always an intriguing exercise. She was not stupidly rigid, but rather, sensibly well organized.

Had she been running the campaign in Spain, Boney's generals would been dusted straight back to France within a year.

She deigned to take up a fork. "I am a trifle hungry."

"And this assuredly does qualify as good food." Saved from plainness by the hint of smokiness from the ham and a tangy quality to the cheese. A peculiar thought crossed Dylan's mind. "Did you wait up for me?"

"Of course not, but on such a night, a caller or two at the back door would not be unusual."

"This late?"

"Not usually, sir. The men would hesitate to disturb your household once the candles are out in the kitchen. Have you heard any more from your sisters about a London visit?"

That maladroit change of subject confirmed that Lydia Lovelace had waited up for him. Dylan was half pleased and half alarmed by such a possibility. In the alternative, perhaps she was plagued by nightmares about cobwebs in the attics.

God knew, Dylan had his share of bad dreams.

"My sisters hint," he said, doing justice to his eggs. "They imply, they don't quite threaten."

"You will please inform me if that changes, sir. One wishes to be in readiness for every eventuality."

Mrs. Lovelace ate with the sort of dainty manners a midnight snack did not merit, but then, Mrs. Lovelace was not the typical housekeeper.

She was younger than the usual exponent of her trade, and not half so substantial. In the better London domiciles, a housekeeper was a general whose influence was felt in orders followed and inspections passed. She did not ruin her knees scrubbing floors or throw out her back hauling baskets of wet laundry. The housekeeper typically had her own parlor, and from her headquarters she deployed the maids and commandeered any unsupervised male employees.

The usual housekeeper was a staff officer, in other words, and seldom found herself in hand-to-hand combat with tarnished candlesticks or dusty carpets. Mrs. Lovelace, by contrast, led her troops by example, perhaps a necessity in a bachelor's modest quarters. Dylan had seen her in the garden laying into the hall runner with a carpet beater, dust flying everywhere.

Close and protracted observation led him to two conclusions regarding Lydia Lovelace. First, she got her hands literally dirty because she did not trust others to do the job right without her example. As an officer, she led the charge rather than hang back while others engaged directly with the enemy.

Second—this insight had only come up on him recently—she maintained a prodigious level of activity in hopes that her fine looks would go unnoticed.

She had lovely dark hair shot through with auburn highlights that became apparent only by candlelight. Her complexion would be the envy of any heiress, her eyes were a gray-green that changed hue with her moods and attire. When she spoke French, Dylan wanted to close his eyes and simply listen to her.

She poured them each a cup of tea and added a dollop of honey to Dylan's cup. "Do you mind about the cat, sir?"

Dylan glanced over at the basket on the hearth, only to find that the calico had been joined by a second calico ball of fluff.

"Kittens, you mean?" Female kittens, which could only lead to the mayhem that passed for feline courtship and to feline progeny.

Mrs. Lovelace stirred her tea with inordinate care. "The pair of them were on the back stoop, Captain. I suspect one of your men brought them around. Nothing on this earth is as pathetic as a wet, bedraggled kitten unless it's two of them. They huddled together, and when I opened the door they should have scampered off, but instead..."

"Instead?" To see the indomitable Lydia Lovelace reduced to explanations wasn't as gratifying as it should have been.

"They looked up at me, all fierce and hopeful, and when I stepped back, they darted into the kitchen. I could not turn them out, sir, but I will take them to the church if you insist."

Dylan sipped his tea, mostly to give himself time to consider options. "You would never allow mice on the premises, Mrs. Lovelace, and those two little wretches are months away from being able to defend the pantries."

She pushed aside her plate of eggs, half the food uneaten. Was she saving it for the cats?

"If you insist, sir, I will make other arrangements for the kittens."

Martyrs accepted their fates in such stoic tones. Dylan had sent men into battle, and led them into near-certain death. If Mrs. Lovelace thought he was incapable of turning out a pair of opportunistic little felines when London's alleys were awash in plump, tasty rodents, she had another—

A hard thumping commenced from the direction of the back door. Dylan was on his feet, mentally reviewing weaponry before the third thump: Knife in each boot, a third knife secured at the small of his back. His walking stick—mahogany, with a brass handle—sat next to the back door.

"Stay out of sight," he muttered. "That's an order, madam." He chose not to take up a carrying candle lest the *visitor* have warning when the door opened.

The pounding continued, slow and determined. Dylan palmed the knife out of his left boot and secreted his hand in the folds his coat. He opened the door and stepped back into the shadows.

A sodden. shivering heap of humanity fell across the threshold. "Thank God. I'm s-s-sorry, Captain, but... th-th-thank God." Private Bowen Brook lay on his back, his features almost unrecognizable beneath blood and bruising. "Hadn't anywhere else t-to go. Sorry."

"Get him out of the wet," Mrs. Lovelace said. "We'll need to remove his clothes and get him warm as soon as may be. Use your knife if you have to."

"These are likely the only clothes he has, and I told you to stay out of sight." Dylan got Brook beneath the arms and dragged him back far enough that Mrs. Lovelace could close the door. "Lad, can you hear me?"

"Aye, sir. I'm right enow. Just got m' bell rung."

Bowen was slight, pale, and half-lame, but like most career infantry, he was amazingly tough. Somebody had done much worse than ring his bell.

"What the hell tempted you onto the streets at such an hour?"

"Interrogate the poor man later," Mrs. Lovelace said, twisting the door lock. "He needs medical attention now."

Gone was the deference of the conscientious housekeeper. In her place stood the general Dylan had long suspected lurked beneath all those lacey caps.

"Best heed her, sir," Bowen said, as Dylan hefted the lad to his feet. "I wouldn't want to get the business end of that poker, if I was you."

Mrs. Lovelace gave Dylan the same sort of look the orphaned kittens had likely given her: Defiant, a little hopeful, quite fierce. She kept a steady grip on a heavy wrought iron poker, too.

Of all the confounded, purely female illogic... She had disobeyed a direct order, *thinking to come to his aid.* But then, an iron poker was a formidable weapon, even in the hands of a smallish woman.

"Come along," Dylan said, securing an arm around Brook's skinny waist. "Mrs. Lovelace does not tolerate insubordination. To the kitchen with you, and you can make the acquaintance of her palace tigers. I'll fetch some brandy from the library, and we'll have you right as a trivet in no time."

Mrs. Lovelace braced Brook from the other side, and he was soon sitting at the kitchen table, the scent of wet wool perfuming the air.

"He'll need dry clothes, Captain," Mrs. Lovelace said, unbuttoning Brook's coat while he sat inert on the chair Dylan had vacated. "Dry socks, the whole lot. I'd run him a hot bath but the water will take too long to heat. When you've fetched the brandy, please bring my medical box from the herbal."

Dylan had been given his orders, a curiously comforting reversal of roles. "Mrs. Lovelace, may I make known to you Mr. Bowen Brook, formerly of the 3rd Bicksford Regiment of Foot. I will return directly." He quick-marched for the steps but paused before ascending. "The kittens can stay, Mrs. Lovelace. I cannot abide the thought of rodents trespassing on your pantry."

She shooed him off, but Dylan's artillery had hit its target. Mrs. Lydia Lovelace had, albeit faintly, smiled *at him*.

ORDER YOUR COPY *MISS DIGNIFIED*!

CPSIA information can be obtained
at www.ICGtesting.com
Printed in the USA
LVHW031218051121
702532LV00027B/2217